HIDD GON

DRAGON RISING SERIES, BOOK 1

TRUDI JAYE

WWW.TRUDIJAYEWRITES.COM

Hi, I'm Trudi Jaye, the author of this book.

If you like *Hidden Dragon*, I think you'll enjoy my other books, too. That's why I'd love you to join my Readers Group.

When you sign up, you'll receive a free novella, plus insider information about Mei and her friends, and deals on my other books.

To become part of my Reader Group, go to:

www.trudijayewrites.com

Hidden Dragon (Dragon Rising Series, book 1)

Published 19 August 2016 by Star Media Ltd

Cover design: PCTC Design

Created with Vellum

With thanks to the SPA Girls. You make writing fun.

1

Si's muscles flex as he swings his long fighting stick toward me.

He looks like an avenging angel; fast and deadly, with no mercy. His short black hair is slicked back off his forehead, and his dark brown eyes are focused on me like he's already planning my death. Mostly those same eyes are wreathed in smiles, with lines crinkling around the edges. But in a fight, he's hard and unforgiving.

To him there's nothing more than to win or lose, to live or die.

Perhaps he's right. I know he's only trying to save me from my enemies.

I block his next attack with my own fighting stick then leap back out of range, landing a quick swipe to his side as I go. Si's expression doesn't change.

I'm sure it hurt like hell—there wasn't enough time to pull up his supernatural defenses—but he's a pro at hiding his emotions.

As for me? I try to hide what I'm thinking, but it doesn't always work. Like right now; sweat's dripping off me, and my legs and arms feel like jelly. We've been at this for a couple hours, and I'm sure my face says exactly what I think of continuing this training session.

But there's no stopping til Si tells me to stop.

Fight and retreat.

Smash and return.

I'm tempted to ask him to call time, but I know I have to fight on. If I give up, Si will make it ten times worse. He's big on lessons that will make me stronger.

Life doesn't just stop because you want it to. If this was a real fight, do you think your enemies would let you take a break?

Si shifts his fighting stick to the other side, his loose cotton trousers swishing as he moves gracefully into a different fighting stance and attacks again—this time slamming his stick toward my midsection.

I block, then attack, kicking one leg high toward his face.

He evades and steps back. "You're not concentrating, Mei. You'll get yourself killed," he says, frowning. His voice is gravelly—some long-ago fight messed with his vocal chords—and it makes him sound grumpy all the time. He was probably defending me, for all I know.

I narrow my eyes and glare at him, but don't reply. I don't know why he's not suffering more from the high intensity training he's been punishing us with. I'm fit and strong, but somehow he's always fitter and stronger.

He's tall and lean, with zero body fat, and a mix of German and Korean ancestry that gives him an unusual look. I've never been able to figure out how old he is, although he's much older than me, of that I'm sure. He's been one of my mentors since I was a little kid, one of the protectors sent to keep me safe from my hunters, but as far as I'm concerned he's always looked exactly the same. With his smooth olive skin and thick dark hair, he could pass for any age between twenty-five and forty-five. Given that he's a supernatural, he could be even older, and I wouldn't be able to tell.

It's his chameleon shifter genes, I guess. He could be two hundred and still look the same age.

A shiver runs along the spell web clinging to my skin, alerting me to another presence nearby; Jeff—my other mentor—has stepped into the training ring alongside Si. The older man might have slowed down with age, but he's a dangerous opponent, and uses whatever tricks he can.

Like surprise, for example.

Luckily I have a secret weapon—my unique link to the spell web that covers all supernaturals makes it impossible for anyone to sneak up on me at close quarters.

I turn, pushing out a back kick, attempting to put Jeff off and give myself a few seconds to prepare for fighting the two of them at once.

Jeff avoids my kick—just—and I feel the movement behind me as Si attacks again.

Sidestepping, I manage to avoid a stick to the head.

I strike out at Si with my stick, landing it against his side, even as I avoid another attack from him.

I twist in midair, landing with a thump, and roll into a low fighting position.

Jeff can't quite keep up with my movements, and I turn fast behind Si to land a kick on Jeff's stomach. He grunts and moves backward.

I take no satisfaction from scoring a point over Jeff. It's like hurting an old faithful dog—a Rottweiler with big teeth, and a nasty streak—but an old dog nonetheless.

Even worse, today he's wearing a lurid Hawaiian shirt instead of his usual dark shirt and tie. He's even got a bit of salt-and-pepper stubble on his face, to go with his slightly longer-than-regulation hair.

He looks like a damn tourist instead of a wily Supernatural Intelligence Group agent.

"You're scared of the new SIG agent," says Jeff, his breath puffing as he tries to recover from my kick. He pronounces each of the letters in the acronym with only a hint of his New York accent. "Maybe he'll be a stickler for the rules. Won't let you go off on your own like I do."

He smirks at me, his bright blue eyes dangerously perceptive.

That's how Jeff wins his fights these days—through mind-fucking his opponent. He's not fast or particularly fit anymore, he's just tough and smart.

And it works.

Despite the fact I *know* it's an attempt to make my emotions take over and put me off, I feel anger and resentment rising up. Jeff's retiring from the SIG. He's quitting his job, *leaving me,* like I'm some damn piece of furniture he doesn't want any more.

Who the hell does he think he is? He doesn't know what I'm feeling.

I take a deep breath and let it out, trying to release my animosity. I narrowly sidestep a punch from Jeff, only to have Si land a solid hit to my leg. Dammit.

My resistance crumbles along with my leg. I stagger to one side, barely escaping another slam from Si's stick. Who am I kidding? I don't want Jeff to go. It feels like I'm losing a limb.

He's the one who figured out how to keep me safe. He's been around a long time; he and Si watched me grow up, looking after scraped knees and drying off my tears, which is more than my real father ever did.

And maybe Jeff's also a little on target. What if the new guy *is* a total jerk? I try to imagine the replacement SIG agent. All I can picture is some starched-up dude in a suit, which is about the last kind of person I want following me around. I can take care of *myself.*

And just like that, Jeff lands a punch to my side and I spin backward. I only just manage to stay on my feet.

"I heard he goes by the rules," Jeff taunts. "Talked to an old friend at the cadet academy. He's fresh out of training and won't want to ruin his chances of promotion."

The words make my hands clench tighter around my fighting stick. Another ripple goes through the spell web and I finally use it in my defense. I reach out along the glowing grid and push a pulse of energy toward Si. He blinks and shakes his head, stepping back out of my range. I can't do the same to Jeff, because he's more human than super, but I hit out at him with my stick.

I'm too distracted to even get close.

Desperately, I try to focus. I know I won't get any points for taking on the two of them at once. Si barely counts Jeff as an opponent these days. The spell web ripples in warning, and Si's weapon slams into my side, knocking the breath out of my lungs with his precise positioning. Where Jeff is all brute strength and trickery, Si is precision and accuracy. I stumble backward, gasping for breath.

Jeff takes the opportunity offered and kicks my legs out from under me. I land on my back; stars fill my vision, and for a millisecond, I wonder what I'm supposed to do. They've got me on the ground, two against one. Si and Jeff loom over me, both waiting for my next move. They're not stupid enough to think I'll stay down.

There's really no question what I'll do next.

Magic.

I seldom use it. Si says it's a crutch and has banned it in the ring. But desperate times...

And Jeff started it. He cheated first.

Water from the nearby fishpond slams into the two men towering over me before either of them knows what's happening. It knocks them both down, pushing them away so I can scramble to my feet. Seconds later, I use my stick to strike three precise hits to both Si and Jeff.

This time Si knows it's coming and has already pulled his protective chameleon scales over his skin, and probably doesn't feel it. Jeff rolls away with a grin, and I can see he's enjoying my response.

I strike again with my stick, directly at his smug expression.

But Jeff's been doing this too long to be caught by a cheeky sideswipe to the head and he ducks back out of range.

"I'm thinking I might not come back, like I planned. I might take a long cruise. Maybe meet someone nice," he says.

Even though I know it's a lie designed to knock me off balance, I still let his words affect me. I stumble and glance toward Jeff. He knows I'm strung out by his impending retirement, and he's using it against me. I wish he'd give it a break sometimes. He's always testing me, trying to make me stronger, unbreakable. Sometimes I wish he'd just say, *well done, you're doing great.*

Instead, Jeff just raises his eyebrows at me. "You better keep an eye on both opponents, Mei. You never know when the other will strike."

Again, a ripple along the spell web alerts me seconds before Si slams his stick into my left thigh. I crumble to the ground, but manage to turn it into a roll at the last minute, and come back to my feet, a little bit away from Si. I turn toward him, ready to take him down once and for all.

Behind me, Jeff speaks again. "I came out to let you know your father's coming tomorrow. He's going to do the debrief himself."

I drop my guard in surprise. My *father*? I haven't seen him since I was four years old. An emotion I can't name grabs hold of my heart. I turn to Jeff again. "What?"

An arm snakes around my neck from behind and pulls me into a lock position, slamming me into the ground and holding my face to the floor. I struggle, but can't break the hold. My concentration is shot; I can't access my magic. Even the spell web feels like it's smothering me. It tingles along my skin, making my magic short circuit.

I'm done.

"Enough," I mutter. "You win." They're cheating, not letting me fight Si properly. They've been doing more and more dirty fighting in the last year. I don't know why I'm surprised every time it happens.

"You can't give up like that," Si says. His voice is inches from my ear. He speaks softly, with only the barest trace of a Korean accent. "You'll die."

"It's not a fair fight. Jeff knows all the buttons to press. I won't be fighting someone who knows that much about me."

"You don't know that. You have to train for all eventualities. It's the only way to survive," Si replies, before letting me go.

"Is he really coming?" I uncurl from my prone position on the ground, but remain seated, my legs crossed.

Jeff hesitates, then nods. "He is. Said he wants to meet this new agent personally."

"He didn't do that when *you* started." I don't remember

much about it, but I'm certain my father didn't come out twelve years ago when Jeff first came on the job.

"Maybe he didn't think you'd make it to twenty at that point," Si says. "There's less than two months to go now. There's more at stake."

I try not to let the words hurt. Si isn't trying to sting me, not like Jeff would have in the ring. He's just stating a fact. What I am means more to my father than who I am. He's not coming to visit with his daughter; he's coming to protect an asset. My father thinks I'm important—not because I'm his daughter, but because of something inside me, something he thinks I can do. This new agent probably means more to him than I do.

I'm not even entirely sure why my father feels so strongly about protecting me. I know I have enemies, people who believe I'm dangerous. They've been trying to kill me from the moment I was born. I don't even know these people, I've done nothing more sinister my entire life than run and hide out. Sometimes I wish I could actually do something to piss off one of my hunters. At least then I'd feel like I had some kind of control over my life.

The irony is, they're all wrong. I don't have anything different or special inside me. At least, no more than every other supernatural out there. The ability to manipulate water, and to sense when someone is coming up behind me on the spell web. I keep waiting for the day they realize it's all a mistake, a miscalculation someone made at my birth. Everything that's special about me has been taught to me by Jeff and Si, through blood, sweat, and tears from the age of eight.

None of it involves magic or an all-consuming power that could destroy the world.

Si extends his hand out to me, and I take it, letting him pull me to my feet. I sigh. "I'm going for a swim."

"Don't be too long. He'll be here soon," Jeff says. There's nothing but concern in his voice now. He's made his point.

I nod, but don't look back as I head along the path between the trees that goes to the river. It might have been part of my training, but Jeff's words are like a thorn under my skin. I need time to lick my wounds and regain my equilibrium.

My steps get faster the closer I am to the water. Soon I'm all but sprinting toward the roar of the waterfall. I emerge out of the forest next to the pool where the river has widened beneath the surging waterfall; the spray hits my body and I let out the breath I didn't know I was holding. As I gaze up at thirty feet of water gushing over the rocks, I can literally feel the power leaking into the air around me. This place has been my savior more times than I can count. It's not just because I have water magic; it's that it soothes me, it envelops me. It shaves off the hard edges of my life and gives me peace again.

I strip down to my bra and panties and start the climb to the top. My body falls into a familiar rhythm, and I let the energy soak into my body, consciously allowing my fears and worries to slip away.

By the time I reach the top, I've almost recovered; I'm clear headed and ready to face anything. I hold my arms out to the side, take a deep breath, close my eyes, and dive over the edge into the water.

2

A long time later, I wander back to the house.

I'm reinvigorated and ready to face whatever they throw at me. I had to put my clothes back on over my dripping body, so I'm a drowned rat version of myself. My shoes squelch as I stride back along the path, and I wish everything wasn't about to change yet again.

I push my magic out along the spell web—the lightly glowing, crisscrossing lines are almost invisible in the sunlight—trying to see if the agent has arrived. Not everyone can use the spell web the way I do—it's like having another set of eyes that can see into the distance and around corners.

Through the spell web, I sense someone else at the house. Not a full supernatural, or even a half, but with strange residual energy that I've never encountered before. As I emerge from the woods, I spot a newish red Ford truck parked in the driveway.

He's here. The new SIG agent, sent to protect me from the countless people who want me dead.

I pause, every instinct pressuring me to run, but I let out

a huff of breath instead. What am I running from? I'm upset because my life is being messed up by circumstances outside of my control; running away will only make it worse. I force myself to stride purposefully toward the back door, but my footsteps slow when I hear raised voices inside.

"What the hell are you talking about?" The stranger's voice is angry, but still manages to have a velvety smooth charm to it. I frown.

"You're the perfect person to be looking after her. I've seen your files." Jeff's voice is calm.

"It's perfect for you, you mean! An older agent looking for a cushy job to finish out his career. This is my first damn assignment! I don't want to be babysitting some helpless girl in the middle of nowhere!"

I shift slightly. Who's he calling helpless?

"This job is important." Jeff's voice doesn't change in tone, but I can tell he's pissed.

"To you! This assignment is going to take me on a fast train to nowhere. You have to take it back." The new agent is pleading now.

"Take what back?"

"Your request to have me here."

"You've got it wrong, boyo, I didn't request you. Special Agent Damien Walker requested you."

There's a long pause. "Walker requested me?" His voice comes out as almost a squeak. I know why. My father is a legend in the Supernatural Intelligence Group. There are even rumors that he doesn't really exist, that he's just a scaremongering tactic used by the agency to keep the other agents in line.

"Yep. And if you'd like to ask him to rescind his request, you can do it yourself. He'll be here tomorrow for your briefing."

"How does he even know who I am?" This time his voice actually does squeak. The velvety smoothness has diminished, and I smirk. That'll teach him for underestimating this assignment.

"We both looked through all the new agents coming out of the cadet training program. You seemed the most qualified."

"But—"

"Yes, I saw the big, black X against your name. We know about the trouble you got yourself into, but that's the kind of out-of-the-box thinking you'll need on this assignment."

"Don't you see? I need a normal assignment. One that will *erase* the black mark, not make it bigger."

"Nothing can erase that mark on your record, son," Jeff says softly. "They'll be watching you for the rest of your life and waiting for you to do it again. Trust me."

"What are you talking about?"

"The same thing happened to me. That's why I ended up here. But it turned out to be the best damn thing that ever happened to me."

Jeff is speaking as if he's just stating a fact, but moisture appears in the corner of my eyes. I don't want Jeff to go. He's more like a father to me than my biological father has ever been.

"Yeah, because it's an easy job," says the new guy.

"You need to stop thinking of this as a cushy assignment." Jeff's voice now has a hard edge to it. "This will be one of the most difficult assignments you'll ever have, if you survive it. In the twelve years I've been here, there have been over five hundred and thirty attempts on her life. Some of those attempts have resulted in the death of Protectors like Si here. Before I came along, three other SIG agents were killed in action. This is not a cushy job, it's just one that I've done well."

There is silence for a heartbeat. "Who is she?"

I hold my breath. This is the question I have asked and asked and asked. They have never given an answer that satisfies me.

"That's classified information," Jeff tells him. "As time goes on, you might reach the right level of security to know more."

I let out a disappointed rush of air.

"How can I protect her if I don't know anything about her?"

"All you need to know is that the Earthbound think she's dangerous. There's also a bounty on her head, so every damn supernatural from here to Timbuktu is your enemy." I hear Jeff pacing around the kitchen, probably getting annoyed at the line of questions.

"What's so special about her?"

"All you need to know is they believe she's a threat to the spell web. They'll do anything to keep her from reaching her full power."

Tingles run along my skin. It's not long now 'til my birthday, and then I'll know for sure who I am and why the crackpots over at the Earthbound compound think I'm so damn dangerous.

"When *does* she turn twenty?" asks the new agent.

"In two months' time."

The new agent whistles low. "So when she reaches the age of maturity, they think she's going to bring down the spell web?"

"They've never come out and told us, but whatever they believe she can do, they want her dead because of it," Jeff clarifies. "It's our job to prevent that."

"What if they're right? What if she *is* a threat to the spell web?"

"When was the last time you saw an actual dragon?" Si enters the conversation for the first time. "Never, that's when. The Dragon Wars were centuries ago. The spell web was created by the Earthbound to rid the world of dragons and their destructive ways. It was successful. They did it. So who is it protecting us from, now? *No one.* We cling to it out of habit rather than necessity."

I hold my breath. That's the most I've ever heard Si say on the subject of the secretive government organization called the Earthbound. Other than knowing they created the spell web, and they want me dead, I've never been able to find out enough about them.

"What makes you so sure you're right about the spell web?" the new agent challenges.

"What makes you so sure I'm wrong?" Si responds softly.

"Whatever you think of the spell web, there's no need to go around killing innocent young girls." The annoyance in Jeff's voice is clear. "The Earthbound have overstepped their boundaries. They've had unlimited reign for so long, they forget they're not always right."

"The SIG—your employers and mine—have a written contract with the Earthbound," says the new agent. "The fact that you and I are here protecting this girl contradicts that agreement."

"Someone higher up than both of us is protecting that girl, and it's not our place to question it," says Jeff.

"Perhaps I should call my supervisor at headquarters—"

I hear Jeff moving, and imagine him getting right up in the new agent's face. "Agent Walker—who outranks us all, including your supervisor—will be here tomorrow," says Jeff, practically growling. "You can ask him every damn question you want about this assignment and the politics of protecting her from the Earthbound. In the meantime, you are strictly forbidden to trumpet her presence to anyone." Jeff's using his SIG agent voice, and I know he's pissed at the new guy for even suggesting he go running to his superiors.

I'm cold and shivering in my damp clothes, so I tiptoe backward and crunch on the gravel outside the door, making my presence known before I open the door and walk into the kitchen.

Three sets of eyes are fixed on me. They all take in my bedraggled appearance. The new agent is a foot taller than Jeff and Si, neither of whom is short. He's got brown hair cut into a regulation hairstyle, and his hazel eyes appraise me warily. Unlike Jeff, who is mostly human from the tips of his toes to the top of his hairy head, this new agent has a patchy covering of the spell web. Not a full glowing grid like Si and I, but enough so I know he has a smattering of supernatural blood in him. I shift slightly, realizing my disheveled state might not be the best way to meet the new agent for the first time. But then again, what the hell do I care? He's already trying to leave.

"Mei, this is Agent Seth Barnes. He's my replacement." Jeff's eyes are unreadable. "Agent Barnes, this is Mei Walker."

Agent Barnes looks at me for a second, blinks, and then turns to Jeff. "She's his *daughter*?" A faint flush appears on his cheeks.

"There's a reason you aced all those exams, isn't there?" Jeff's words are delivered with a bite. "Yes, she's his daughter."

Agent Barnes runs one hand shakily through his hair. "There's no way I can get out of this damn assignment, is there?"

Jeff shakes his head. "Not without ruining your career."

I glance back and forth between them. A shimmering anger heats my skin, and I have to force myself to take deep breaths. "If you've finished talking about me as if I'm not here, I'll be going." I turn and stalk off in the direction of my room. I need to take a shower anyway. I'm not interested in getting to know this new guy if he's already written me and this assignment off.

"Mei! Come back here."

Ignoring Jeff, I slam the door to my room; I'm too annoyed to be polite. Real mature, I know, but it's not like I want this new guy here anyway. He's acting like he's the one who's been put-upon. What about me? I'm the one who's constantly guarded, watched and fussed over. Forever living in fear of having the most powerful supernaturals on the planet find and kill me for some lame reason I don't even understand. How on earth could I destroy the spell web? Even if I could, why would I want to? I like the spell web. It makes me feel safer knowing it's there.

Every supernatural knows the story. Three hundred years ago, the planet was overrun with dragons. They fought desperate and bloody battles for territory, killing hundreds of thousands of humans and supernaturals. The devastation was beyond anything seen since, including any of the human wars.

The spell web was how a small secret society called the Earthbound defeated the dragons and saved the planet. We've been covered by it, and they've been the heroes of the supernatural people, ever since.

I shiver. I was seven when one of my Protectors, Lee, noticed the way I was talking about the spell web and asked me to explain. When I told him I saw the web as a glowing grid over all the supernaturals we came across, his expression became fearful. I still remember the soft words he spoke.

Never tell anyone else what you can do, Mei. No one else can see it like that. It's not the kind of power the SIG would ever want you to have.

His words scared me so much, I never told anyone else. When Lee was killed, my secret died with him. I sometimes think Si and Jeff suspect, but they've never asked and I've never told. Being able to see it and use it to my advantage is one big reason why I'd never want to get rid of the spell web. It's another sense I use, like taste and touch, that helps me through my day. It'd be like cutting off an arm. No, more like cutting off *all* my limbs.

Pulling off my damp clothes, I head to the shower, the edge of my anger already wearing off. As usual, the warm water soothes me, caressing my body in just the right way, and allows my brain to sort through the information I've just overheard. Most of it isn't new.

Of course there is one piece of information that sticks out. I keep going back to it, trying to unpack it in my head. *They think I might bring the spell web down.*

Although this has never been explicitly stated to me before, I'd guessed it already. It makes sense; it's the main responsibility of the Earthbound. I rub my arms fiercely with the soap, making frothy bubbles along my skin.

The way I see and use the spell web is unique. I've researched my ability, all the way back to when the original spell was instigated, but I can find no mention of it. The Earthbound—who were just a ragtag group of secretive radical supernaturals back then—went to the ruling Supernatural Council and told them they could destroy the dragons by creating a spell. It was designed to cover the physical bodies of every single supernatural on the planet, including the dragons. The spell would then absorb a portion of each supernatural's magic in order to supply the energy needed to control the dragons. Using the spell web, the Earthbound were able to not only defeat the dragons, but to run them to the ground and kill them off completely.

I chew on my lip. Si is right. Everyone knows dragons are extinct. Why do we still need the spell web? I rub one hand over the gently glowing grid visible on my arm, wondering how much more powerful I'd be if I didn't have it constantly over me like a tight Lycra suit. I shake my head. I don't care.

They think I want it gone?

The very thought sends terrified shivers along my body.

3

"Mei!" Jeff's voice carries down the hallway and into my room.

I sigh and stand up. I'm going to have to face the music eventually—this isn't something I can put off. I slowly walk down the hallway and back into the living room, running one hand along the wall as I go. They're all sitting on the sofas and glance up at me as I enter the room. Si and Jeff look comfortable, almost smug. Agent Barnes, on the other hand, does not. He's sitting stiffly, both hands on his knees. His face looks pale against the dark blue of the suit he's wearing. I'm betting his discomfort is mostly because he's being set upon by two masters of psychological warfare. He probably has no idea what's happening.

"I need you to take Agent Barnes into the village, show him around. Help him get acclimatized."

I blink, startled. "I don't—"

"Surely you'd—"Agent Barnes says at the same time.

We both stop. I narrow my eyes at him.

"Mei, you know where the keys are. Take Bertha out.

And use the old track. I don't want too much traffic on the new driveway in one day."

I roll my eyes, but go to the counter where the keys are hanging within easy reach. "Come on, Agent Barnes. We may as well do as they say. They'll only harass us until we do."

He stands up, his tall frame looming over us all as he looks uncertainly from Jeff and Si to me. I raise my eyebrows at him. He firms his lips and gestures for me to lead the way, but his hazel eyes are burning.

I lead him to the garage at the side of the house, opening the door wide so he can see Bertha. He stops in midstride and starts shaking his head; I take a moment to enjoy his expression. The truck has seen better days—she looks like an old rust-bucket on the outside—but Si keeps her tuned to an inch of her life, so she's as reliable as any vehicle can be.

"Come on. It's fine," I say impatiently.

"We should go in my truck."

I shake my head. "Too noticeable. It's bright red."

"This is pretty distinctive too. It's a pile of junk."

"Everyone has trucks like this around here. Bertha's designed to fit in."

He sighs, but climbs up into the cab beside me, and pulls on the seatbelt.

I can't help myself, I grin at him. "It's okay, you'll be fine."

"Are you even old enough to drive?" he asks.

I blink uncertainly and then frown. I look young, I know that. It's because I'm short as well as slight. It's handy when you're on the run, because people tend to overlook you, but Agent Barnes knows exactly how old I am. He's just being an ass. I turn the key, put the truck into gear, and roar out of the garage, spewing gravel over his nice tidy truck as I go. I execute a perfect turn and then speed off down the lesser-known 'old track' that Jeff referred to.

I keep the speed up, bouncing over potholes, holding tightly onto the steering wheel, and making sure I bounce him around as much as possible. A couple of times his head hits the roof of the cab, and he has to slouch down to keep it from happening again.

"Okay, okay, I get your point," he says eventually. "Can you please slow down now?"

"I don't know what you're talking about," I say, as I go over another particularly big pothole.

His head hits the roof of the cab again, and he swears. "Stop it! I'm sorry for suggesting you were too young to drive."

"And what about everything else? Do you apologize for talking about me like I wasn't there? And for trying to leave the assignment before it's even begun?"

He turns to look at me. "Look, it's nothing personal. I don't know you, or anything about you, but this is my first assignment out of the cadet academy. I can't be stuck babysitting in the middle of nowhere like this."

I'm stung by the babysitting comment, but manage to swallow it down. "We don't live here, you know," I say. "We constantly move around." This is Si's private retreat, so we come back here whenever we get a chance, but it's the first time I've been here in over a year.

"Really?" He raises his eyebrows. "Is that how he's kept you safe for so long?"

I hold my lips around the information that the main way Jeff has kept me safe is by teaching me to take care of myself. He's been teaching me survival techniques since he met me when I was seven years old. He also insisted that Si start training me in the super-secret martial art used by the Protectors at around the same time. "Sure. Moving around helps. Not too much, not in the same pattern every time, sometimes in one place for a few months, sometimes for only a few weeks or even days."

Agent Barnes nods. "That makes sense."

"It's one tactic." I prefer the times we've stayed in one place for months on end. To me it's easier to defend somewhere stable, but Jeff doesn't like any of us to become too complacent. He says it's not good for my health.

"You don't approve?"

"There are other ways to defend against threats. And by moving around, we're exposing ourselves to more people." I shake my head. It doesn't matter what I think. Jeff is the one leading my security team. At least until tomorrow.

"You only need to be concerned about the supernaturals, surely?" Agent Barnes glances at me, his hazel eyes studying my face.

I blink and focus my gaze on the track in front of me, suddenly feeling hot all over. "Sure. Humans are obviously unaware of the Earthbound bounty on my head, or even that there's anything strange going on. The spell web works for me in that way." I have always been a talker when I get nervous. I have to clamp my lips shut to keep from saying anything more.

"Did you know that it wasn't on purpose?"

"What wasn't?" I frown and glance at him, forgetting my determination to keep my eyes on the road.

"The part of the spell web that keeps humans from seeing anything to do with supernaturals," he says, gesturing toward me. "How the humans forgot supernaturals even existed as soon as the spell web covered the world. The Earthbound created the spell web with the sole purpose of destroying the dragons, and the supers agreed because there was no other way at the time. But no one, not the supernaturals nor the Earthbound, cared whether humans knew about supernaturals. It was just an unintended side effect they discovered after the spell web was in place."

"You have to admit it's helpful."

"I think Agent Harvey and your Protector Si might disagree with you."

For a moment, I'm confused—I have no idea who this Agent Harvey might be. And then I realize he means Jeff. "Jeff talks a lot. It can be hard to figure out what he really thinks."

"Both Agent Harvey and the Protector seem pretty clear to me."

"It doesn't matter what they think. The Earthbound are in charge of the spell web, and they're not going to let it come down any time soon."

He shrugs and turns back to the road. We're almost to the end, and when I turn onto the main highway, he relaxes slightly. We drive in silence, and we soon arrive at the small town of Keepsake, population five hundred and seven. I park in front of the grocery store and get out of Bertha's cab. "You coming in?" I ask.

He levers himself out of the truck and stands, towering over me by at least a foot and a half. His face is a mask now, and he's looking up and down the street, the way Jeff does when he's assessing the threats around us. I've already done it, and I'm happy to report there's nothing shady going on in Keepsake today.

Walking into the store, I keep my head down. I recognize a few of the locals but only because I've been coming regularly. We make a point of avoiding contact with people in general. It could get them hurt.

I pick up the supplies that Jeff has asked me to get; flour, rice, and a few fresh veggies. That's another reason to stay in one place, we'd be able to grow our own vegetables. Agent Barnes follows me around like a shadow, saying nothing.

"That all for today, love?" Margie—according to her name badge—asks. She glances at Agent Barnes behind me, and then away. Something about him makes her nervous.

I smile. "That's it, thanks."

As she's ringing up our purchases, she hums softly to herself. I recognize the tune. It's from Jeff's favorite Beach Boys album. The song is "Good Vibrations".

Suddenly a shiver goes down my spine. There's a buzzing in my ears, and I sway where I'm standing.

Something is wrong.

I drop the handles of the grocery bag I was about to lift from the counter, and sprint out of the store. Margie calls after me, but I ignore her.

"What the hell are you doing?" Agent Barnes yells, as he sprints behind me. When I jump in the truck and start the engine, he leaps too, only just getting the door closed as I reverse the truck out of the parking lot and onto the road.

"Something's wrong. There's something wrong," I manage to say. It's all along the spell web now. It's shimmering along my arms, all lit up like a birthday cake. There's anticipation in there, but also a manic kind of expectation. There's murder in the spell web today.

I speed back along the highway.

"Tell me what's happening. What is wrong?"

"I can... I can feel it. Through my magic." Even now, I

don't mention my connection to the spell web. I try to see through the trees and up to the old mountain cabin where Jeff and Si are about to be attacked. For once, I curse Jeff's insistence on no mobile phone for me. Too easy to trace. I glance at Agent Barnes. "Do you have a phone?"

He nods, pulling it out. He starts dialing a number.

"Tell Jeff there are multiple supers coming. They'll be there soon. They need to get out of there."

As Jeff answers the phone, I can hear the sound of gun shots in the background. I ram my foot down on the accelerator until it will go no further, and the old truck responds smoothly. Si knows what he's doing with cars.

Agent Barnes puts his phone on speaker, and I can hear Jeff swearing. "Barnes, you get her away from here. There are too many of them. We're trapped. Don't you dare let her come back here."

"We're on our way, Jeff," I say calmly, ignoring his words. "We'll be there soon."

"No, damn you, Mei. You run from here, right now. Promise me."

I shake my head. "You know better than to think I'd leave you like this. We're coming."

"Mei, listen to me for once! This is more than even you can handle. We'll meet you at the usual place. You get Agent Barnes to take you to our usual meeting point." In the background, I can hear a crash and the sound of more shooting. Then the line goes dead.

"You heard him. Turn the truck around. We can go to this meeting place and wait for them." Agent Barnes looks at me expectantly.

I know, even if the agent doesn't, that Jeff doesn't think he'll be meeting me at the usual place. There's no way I'm going to the meeting place to wait like an idiot. I swerve off the road and onto the old track. The tires screech, and for a split second, control of Bertha slips from my fingers. Time slows and I hold my breath, using the spell web to pull us back into place. Then I'm heading up the old rutted track, pounding over the potholes, driving like my life depends on it.

"What are you doing? We had a direct order. Turn around at once." Agent Barnes is holding tight to the side and dashboard of the truck.

"He's not my boss."

"The primary mission is to keep you safe. Turn around now!" He tries to pull at the steering wheel. I slam my elbow into his chest. I might be small, but I pack a punch and he retreats, rubbing his chest and trying to breathe through the winding I've just given him.

"If you try to stop me again, I'll do something more permanent." I keep my eyes focused on the road ahead of me, and slow down when we get within a mile of the house. I'm not so lost to reason that I'm going to go charging in making all the noise I can. "We go on foot from here." And when I say go on foot, I mean sprint as fast as we can. I grab the handgun and bullets from the glove compartment.

I'm off and running across the grassy field next to the truck before Agent Barnes even gets out of the car. He's still having a little trouble breathing after my elbow to his chest. Up ahead, the sound of guns permeates the air. I'm relieved. If it had been silent, it would have been all over. I race into the forest behind the house with Agent Barnes wheezing behind me.

Within minutes, I'm hiding out in the trees at the far side of the house. Crawling through the undergrowth, I see at least three targets. I shoot, and two go down before anyone realizes I'm shooting. I blend back into the bushes and race around to the front of the house.

A body is lying beside Agent Barnes's truck. I don't pay much attention at first, but then I notice the Hawaiian shirt.

Jeff.

All the air goes out of my lungs and I struggle to breathe.

It's fine. He's just unconscious.

Without looking, I run to Jeff, crouching down beside him. I have to get him out of here, get him some medical attention.

I turn him over, murmuring to him, telling him it's going to be okay. My eyes are drawn to the large red stain spreading over his shirt. It's just a scratch. I'm sure he's fine. I reach with shaking fingers to his neck, trying to find a pulse.

Someone grabs me from behind, and I automatically slam my elbow backward. I turn, and it's a stranger gasping for breath behind me, dressed all in black. I snarl at him, kicking out in three efficient strikes from my right leg. He falls to the ground with a broken neck. I turn, almost eager for my next target.

Another figure runs in my direction, and I lean into my stance, ready to fight. To kill. I've forgotten my gun in favor of the punishing need for physical revenge.

Then I recognize the tall man striding toward me, his gun out and his hazel eyes intent on me. Agent Barnes. "He's dead," I blurt out. "They killed him." My voice wavers, and I clear my throat, pushing down the emotion that wants to burst out. I have to find Si. "Have you seen the rest of them?"

"They're around the other side. Come on." Agent Barnes grabs my arm and drags me back to the forest at the side of the house. We crawl under the cover of the trees and low bushes until we see what's happening on the other side.

A group of men are crowded together. As one man

moves to the side, I see Si on his knees in front of a man with a hand gun. Si shakes his head in the negative. A shot rings out, and Si falls to the side, landing in a crooked heap. For a moment, I can't do anything.

Then I start screaming.

4

I don't know how he does it, but Agent Barnes convinces me to run.

We slam our way blindly through the trees, even as the sounds of our pursuers follow us. I shouldn't have screamed. I know better. But losing them both in one day is too much. It's more than I can bear.

"Don't let them die in vain," he says as I start to slow down.

All I can see is the blood pooled around Jeff's body, his glassy eyes staring up at me, and the way Si jerked as the bullet hit before he fell limply to one side.

Everything gone in one fell swoop. I want to curl up on the forest floor and sob.

From behind, Agent Barnes pushes me roughly forward, not giving me an option. So I run toward the only thing that feels safe—the waterfall. We're crashing through the underbrush, no thought to being quiet. There would be no use. At the sound of my scream, every single eye in the whole place had turned to look at me.

And now they're all running after us.

A shot fires, and I feel the rush of wind past my face. I inhale sharply, but I'm not scared. I'm beyond that. If I didn't have Agent Barnes behind me pushing me along, I think I might have considered making a last stand.

Could I beat all of them?

I'm a pretty good shot, and I know how to fight. But I don't think I could win against so many of them, especially if Si and Jeff couldn't manage it. The point is that I don't want to live. Not if it means living without the two men who have been with me, looking out for me, for as long as I can remember. My only family has just been killed.

My real family, that is.

I'm tempted by the idea of stopping. But by sheer will, Agent Barnes keeps me running, his large form behind me, urging me on like nothing else could have.

Crashing through the last of the trees and undergrowth, we come out at the waterfall pool. It sparkles in the sunlight as if nothing is happening. Another shot goes off, and Agent Barnes grunts behind me, falling onto my back.

I lose my footing at the edge of the pool, and we both plunge into the water below. I'm sinking fast, the dead weight of Agent Barnes pushing me down. I hit the bottom of the pool, scraping my cheek against a rock as Agent Barnes' limp body settles heavily on top of me.

I panic, bubbles escaping from my mouth as I try to move him off me before I need to breathe. He's heavy, but I'm wily. I also have water magic, when I remember to use it. A few seconds later, I manage to twist out from under him, struggling to keep my breath steady underwater. I push back up to the surface to catch my breath, then dive back down.

The water has been stained red, making it hard to see, but I catch a glimpse of the agent's body in the depths below. Using my strength and the water around me, I kick down and grab hold of his shirt, pulling with all my might. I don't know if he's alive or dead, but I'm not going to leave him behind.

I've seen too many deaths today.

I don't know if our pursuers are up there or not, so I use the last of my breath to swim underwater, dragging his body behind me, until I'm under the spray from the waterfall. The cave behind has always been another of my sanctuaries. I break the surface and manage to push Barnes up onto the narrow ledge, while I cling to the rocky side of the pool. I can see a bullet wound through his shoulder and I let out a breath of relief. Surely he can survive a wound to the shoulder?

I rip off a piece of my T-shirt and hold it against the wound. Barnes groans and his eyes flutter open. "It's going to be okay," I say, more to myself than to him. I'm starting to shiver and I don't know if it's from the cold or because of what I've just seen.

"We need to get out of here," he gasps, trying to lever himself up.

I push him back down again. "There's nowhere to go." I can hear shouting outside from the men who killed Si and Jeff.

I turn and consider the wall of water that's cascading down between us. Gently, I push magic at the water, making it a thicker, stronger barrier. I don't know if it's going to help, but I've never been happier to have an affinity for water.

Turning back to my patient, I wonder what the hell we're going to do. We can't stay hidden here forever.

Harsh voices calling out from both sides of the waterfall pool make me flinch. They've arrived at the waterfall.

"Which way did they go?"

"I can't see them."

"Look, there's blood in the water. Down that way."

"She's got water magic. They probably swam downstream."

Footsteps run off into the distance, and I let out a sigh of relief. Beside me, Agent Barnes groans.

Looking at him from my position in the water, I consider my options. He's in a lot of pain. He's not going to be able to walk or run very far. The truck may as well be a million miles away at this point. I need to find some way to heal his wounds and get us out of here, and I don't have the first clue.

All I can see is the blood on Jeff's chest and his blank eyes staring out at me. A part of me wants to just sink down into the water and never come back up. My life has always been a battle to survive. It would be nice to feel at peace, to have silence and calm surrounding me. My fingers unclench around the rocks at the side, and I start slipping down.

Then Agent Barnes coughs, a painful sound that jolts me back to life. It's about more than just me at the moment. I have to help him.

Healing has never been my strength; Si says it's because I'm too impatient.

The healing arts are about taking tiny little steps, forging a connection between millions of miniature cells so they can band together again in the right way. Putting them together in the wrong way is the direct route to more harm, and often death. It's a fine line, and one I don't want to walk.

But I have to try something.

I pull myself up onto the ledge next to his head, looking down at his ashen face. First things first. Sending feelers along the spell web, I attempt to sense his wounds using his connection to the spell web. But his coverage is sporadic at best, and he's only got a tiny bit of magic.

When I try to push some of my magic into his wound, he

groans, and it doesn't seem to change anything. I take heart from the fact that some color has returned to his face. Hopefully that will be enough for now.

"Do you think you can walk?" I asked him.

He shakes his head. "We should wait till nightfall. There are too many of them."

"Did you get a head count?"

"Twelve at least." He hesitates. "Plus the three you killed." His expression is carefully bland.

"They were attacking my home. It was self-defense." I shift my position on the narrow ledge. It's not the first time I've had to kill someone attacking my home and family, but it doesn't come easily to me.

"I wasn't judging. It was just... unexpected."

What he doesn't say is that he'd thought I was a useless little girl he'd have to babysit. I glare at him. "It's Jeff's way of making sure I'll be all right, whatever happens." I barely get the last couple of words out before dissolving into tears.

The day Jeff was preparing for has arrived.

Bang.

A shot goes off in the distance, and I jerk. I rub my hands up and down my bare arms, wishing I had a sweater with me. "There's a safe house not far from here. If we can get to the truck, we can hole up there for a few days until you feel better."

Agent Barnes shakes his head. "We need to let someone know what's happened. Agent Walker, my supervisor, someone."

I shrug. "If you like. But they've never been much help in the past." Not even my father.

He pulls out his phone and tries to dial, but it's dead. The plunge into the water was too much for it.

"Do you have a phone?"

I shake my head. "Jeff didn't like how easily they could be traced. He tried to avoid them if at all possible. And he and Si didn't want me to rely on them." I shrug. It wouldn't have survived the dip in the water any more than Agent Barnes's phone had anyway.

He swears and then groans in pain.

"Right now none of that matters," I say soothingly. "We'll call this in later. Just try to get some rest until dark. I'll keep watch."

Agent Barnes glares at me, but he's obviously exhausted and eventually closes his eyes and settles back into the rock floor.

I lean back against the rock wall behind me, gaining some solace from the powerful flow of water that's protecting us from the outside world.

I've lived with the knowledge that people have died for me my whole life. Si told me once that my mother even died defending me when I was just a baby. Si's brother protectors were all killed, most recently Lee when I was twelve.

But Jeff and Si had given me a sense of security these last twelve years. I'd been feeling safe and comfortable.

Now, I realize how false that feeling of safety really was.

5

I'm sitting, staring at the water when I start to wonder how they found us at Si's hideout. This location should have been secure. We'd worked long and hard at it, with not only every evasive maneuver that Jeff could think of in his special agent repertoire, but also with various spells and protective charms.

Plus, the crazy backtracks and sidetracks we use to get here, not to mention the false names. Agent Barnes hadn't known the final location until he was a couple miles out. In fact, everything that could be done to protect Si's house, had been done.

So how did they know?

There was only one person who could have led them to us. Only one change in our normal routine. I turn and to stare at Agent Barnes lying prone on the ledge beside me. He shakes his head from side to side in his sleep, seeming to deny my thoughts. I'm tempted to agree. He looks too young and naive to have been part of such a plot.

My hands clench at my sides. His whole dissatisfied

agent act could have been just that—an act, a ploy to distract us from the fact he'd led the Earthbound right to us. He argued with Jeff and Si about the assignment, about the spell web, about being here. He caused a distraction so we wouldn't pay as much attention to other possible issues.

And now Jeff and Si were dead.

My gaze lands on the phone he's still clutching in one hand. He was so keen to ring his supervisor and had been upset when he discovered the phone was dead. Had he been planning to let them know where we are? My lips press together into a single hard line. I'm prepared to kill him right here and now if he had any part in their deaths. Leaning forward, I consider the ways I'd make him pay.

As I'm watching his face scrunch up in pain, and it's hard to imagine anyone taking a bullet for the sake of some ploy. He moves restlessly, and the dampness of the waterfall hideaway rises up around us. I tentatively send a query via the spell web, unsure if his weak and broken covering will tell me anything more about him. At first I struggle to make sense of it; his spell web is confusing at best. The patterns eventually emerge and I begin to travel along his grid lines, hopefully seeking something that will tell me if he's part of this.

It's not long before I find it. A tiny tracking spell stuck deep inside his body where no one would think to look. Disbelief and anger rise in equal measures. It was him. He led these people to us.

Why didn't Jeff consider this possibility earlier? We should have met Agent Barnes at a neutral location instead of allowing him to come all the way into our favorite secure location.

I edge away from him, not sure what to do. First things first. I need to know if he did this intentionally. He's in pain, and he's not himself. But it's his fault that Jeff and Si are dead, so my sympathy is at a low ebb. Figuring out how deep in this mess he is will help me decide whether I leave him here with a second bullet through his skull or take him with me when I go.

I hold one hand over his bullet wound. I hesitate, but gathering my anger around me like a cloak, I push my hand down over the entry point.

He screams, his whole body jerking upward. His eyes pop open, and he stares at me with pain-glazed eyes. "What are you doing?" he gasps.

"You led them here. You have a tracking spell inside you."

"What?" He shakes his head. "No. No. That's not true." His face has returned to the waxy paleness that he had earlier. Sweat appears on his forehead.

Determined to punish him, I push harder. "If you want to survive the next five minutes, you need to tell me the truth."

He shakes his head quickly, his eyes wild. "I did... exactly what... I was told to do. I wouldn't... lead killers here." His words come out in gasps, and he's shaking.

"Not even if it was the Earthbound? You argued with Jeff about it."

He coughs and swallows over dry lips. "I didn't know who... you were. I was told... it was a protection job... in the middle of nowhere."

I scan his features, trying to spot a lie. Jeff is better at reading people than me.

You have to assume they're lying and work from there, Mei.

"What are you lying to me about?" I push on his wound to emphasize my point.

He groans, and his head falls limply to one side. I've

managed to make him pass out. A part of me feels remorse. I'm hurting him on purpose, but I need to know if I can trust him. Reaching into the water, I gather a small handful and pour it over his head. He sputters and his eyes flick open again.

"What are you lying to me about?" I ask again, not daring to punctuate my question with another jab at his bullet hole.

He shakes his head. "Nothing." He hesitates, breathing heavily. "I was told... to make my way up here. I... I thought it was punishment for... something I did... at cadet training." His face is flushed and he's gasping for air. I don't think he knows anything more than he's saying.

"Who sent you up here? Who is your supervisor?" It had to be someone Jeff felt he could trust. I run through the SIG agents Jeff has spoken about, in my mind. It has to be one of them and luckily for me, it's not a very long list. Whoever it is, I'm going to find them and make them pay.

He shakes his head. "Can't tell you... Classified."

"Whoever they are, they didn't think twice about sending you into this operation."

He blinks. "What are you talking about?"

"You're supposed to be dead. You're the dummy in the middle who ends up with all the blame."

Agent Barnes shakes his head. "No."

"The Earthbound knew our location. They followed a tracking spell inserted inside you. If it wasn't you, it must have been someone at SIG headquarters."

"That makes no sense. They would just call you in if they were going to hand you over to the Earthbound. There's no need for all this..." He spreads his hand out to indicate the men hunting them.

I shake my head. "This is a rogue agent. Someone who's

working against the SIG's directive to protect me." I narrow my eyes at Agent Barnes. "And it better not be you."

Agent Barnes moves restlessly, his face showing his distress. He's bleeding again. I need to get him medical attention, or he's not going to make it. I glance guiltily down at the widening stain of red on his shirt.

I'm not entirely sure he's innocent in this, but I don't want him to die. At least not until I know if he deserves it.

"We're going to have to make a run for the truck. But first I'm going to try to heal your wound a little." I just have to hope that Si was wrong about my healing skills.

He nods.

Taking in a deep breath, I use the water next to us to gather energy. My hand slips down into the restless pool, and I close my eyes. I skim along the spell web, using it to enter his body. I can feel the wound with my other senses, the smell of the thick, red blood thumping through his veins, the reedy sound of his gasping breaths as he tries to keep calm.

The first thing I realize is that the bullet is lodged inside his body still. I hesitate for a moment, but I'm pretty sure it needs to come out. The temptation to use my fingers and dig inside him is huge, but I decide to try with magic first. It will be better if I can push it out without causing too much harm.

I send out tendrils of magic, so light and wispy you might think you imagined them. Taking a couple deep breaths, I gather the tendrils around the metal of the bullet and pull.

Agent Barnes screams, and I jerk back, almost losing my place on the ledge and falling into the water. As it is, I scrape my hand, and drops of blood form on my palm.

So much for the soft and gentle approach. I sit back up,

and consider my options.

I don't have many.

I close my eyes again, form the connection with his body, and send my magic out to hover over him. In one deep, sharp thrust, I shove my magic inside his body and drag the bullet out. Agent Barnes screams again and passes out. The bullet emerges easily and pops into my waiting hand.

I glance back at the wall of water behind us, hoping my spell and the noise of the waterfall will coincide to ensure his screams weren't heard by our hunters.

Next I look for the tracking spell. We can't go anywhere with that thing still inside him. I race along his spell web, jumping over the broken bits until I find the tiny little spell that destroyed my life. I slam enough magic into it to break it apart a thousand times, my grief fuelling my magic. Agent Barnes groans but doesn't wake.

When I check again, the tracking spell is gone. Just like Jeff and Si. I'm shaking so hard I see ripples in the spell web across my skin.

I force my thoughts back to Agent Barnes and attempt the healing magic Si has been teaching me. It's about tiny increments, and I have to focus my whole attention on moving the tiny cells I can't see. It's difficult work, and I'm not confident I've made much headway until the agent blinks open his eyes; his gaze is clearer and more focused. The bleeding seems to have stopped and the wound is gaping less than before.

I sigh with relief. It's not perfect, but it will do until I can find a proper healer.

"Thank you," he whispers.

"Don't thank me yet. We've still got to get to the truck. You'll be swearing at me by the time we get there." I smile down at him, trying to soften my words, but I mean it. He's going to find it difficult to move, let alone run like I'm going to make him.

6

We're about halfway to the truck, the agent's arm draped over my shoulders and his blood dripping down my shirt, when I hear the shouts of our pursuers. I don't think they've seen us. The forest is hiding us and it's dark, with clouds covering the moon and stars.

But they're close.

I speed up, knowing we only have a small window of time. I'm glad he's almost unconscious now, because he'd wonder how someone as small as I am can carry a big guy like him. Or maybe he wouldn't. He's an SIG agent, after all.

We make it to the edge of the forest. The truck is only just visible in the distance; all I can really see is a large shape on the track, but my heart lifts.

We're going to make it.

I shift Agent Barnes across my shoulder, and tread carefully along the forest's edge, trying to get as close as I can to the vehicle before I have to step out into the open. My eyes are focused on the blue truck; everything inside me is directed like a bullet toward making it there. By force of will, I'm going to get us out of this situation.

When I see someone covered with the glowing spell web wander around one side of the truck, I stumble and almost fall flat on my face.

Barnes groans incoherently. I can make out a rifle in the man's arms and he's big. Pausing beside a tree, I lean Agent Barnes against the trunk and crouch down, peering around the edge. Another man joins the first, again with his spell web glowing, and my heart pounds in my chest. I'm going to have to fight for the truck.

Standing up again, I pull Barnes to his feet, taking most of his weight on my shoulders. I keep moving through the trees, staying low. I don't have perfect night vision, but it's okay. This time I'm careful to keep us well out of sight. Luckily, I'm wearing black, and Agent Barnes has a dark blue suit over a black shirt.

It doesn't hurt that I have one more advantage over them. I can see and use the spell web against them.

When I'm about thirty yards from the truck, I settle Agent Barnes against a tree. He mumbles something that I can't hear, and then slumps to one side. This escape has been hard on him, but we can't stop now.

I'm going to have to race to Bertha, trying to stay unnoticed in the field of long grass. I rub one shaking hand down my trouser leg. I don't know why I'm so nervous. They can't possibly be more difficult to fight than Si. They're just bigger and meaner looking. I wait until they're both on the other side of the truck, and take off in a crouching run.

Moments later, I'm hiding on the other side of my truck, listening hard. All I can hear is the pounding of my heart and the scratchiness of my dry throat as I swallow. The moon comes out from behind the clouds, bathing the truck and road in silvery light, and I curse under my breath. The cover of darkness is an asset to me right now. But I don't have a choice.

I take a breath and step out in front of the truck. "You looking for someone?" I ask, trying to smile casually. It feels more like a grimace.

One of the men jumps and turns, his rifle pointed straight at my chest. I try not to squirm. The other spins slowly, a smile spreading across his broad face. He's got beady eyes that seem too bright. "The boss was right," he says. "It *is* our lucky day."

I stand in front of them, loose limbed and relaxed, content for them to feel like they're in charge.

"Don't move a muscle, little lady, and you won't get hurt. Much." The bright-eyed man walks toward me, his rifle held protectively in front of him.

I know my way around weapons—Jeff saw to that—but Si insists they make people lazy. *As soon as they get behind a gun, people feel invincible*, he always says. Looking at these two guys, I see he's right.

At least, he *was* right. A lump appears in my throat and a burning sensation rises up through my chest. I focus my anger on these two men. They think they have an edge over me. I'm going to see if it's true.

Loosening my legs, I bounce lightly on the front pads of my feet. The movement doesn't seem to bother the two men unduly, but it should. I'm preparing for a fight.

"Keep your gun on her. I'm gonna to tie her up," says Bright-Eyes. The other man comes closer, still holding the gun on me; he's got the thick lips and the slightly squishy walk of a water creature. I run my magic along his spell web and discover he's got so much liquid inside his body, I can hold him just using my water magic.

As Bright-Eyes steps in close to grab my arm, I strike out. Three moves later—one kick and two punches—I have his weapon, and he's down on the ground, groaning. A couple of yards away, the water-creature is straining his body in all directions, but standing stock-still. I have him tightly wound up inside my magic. I stride over and take his gun, allowing my magic to settle, and then throw two quick punches to knock him out. He hits the ground with a satisfying thud.

It wasn't even a decent fight, but it does make me feel better to hit someone.

I turn back to the first guy and grab the rope he was planning to use on me. Dragging their bodies to the side of the gravel road, I tie them to each other. I'm hardly even puffing by the time I've done all this.

Si has been training me hard for the last twelve years.

Picking up their guns, I put them in the truck. The clouds move over the moon again and the night darkens around me. Glancing around, I can't see anything, but it feels like someone is breathing down my neck. There are other hunters out here, looking for us, and if they could get the better of Si and Jeff, they can almost certainly take me out. Our only advantage is the night.

I run back to where I left Barnes. He's still passed out. I heft him up over my shoulders and jog back across the long grass. It takes longer than I'd like to get him in the truck, and I'm glancing around anxiously by the time I'm done. He's all buckled up, but only semi-conscious and slumps against the door as I close it.

Jumping into the truck, I turn it around and accelerate down the track. I have to keep the lights off, which makes it almost impossible to see the road, and I hunch over the wheel like a grandma, peering out into the darkness. Like I said, my night vision isn't amazing and the moon is completely hidden by clouds now. I'm relying on my memory of the track to keep us safe.

The bumping brings Agent Barnes around, and he turns his head, trying to figure out what's happening. "We made it to the truck?" he says with surprise in his voice.

I shrug. "Now we just need to make it to the bottom of this track."

He sits up straighter and sees the guns. "You ran into someone?"

I nod.

"Are they alive?"

I ignore his question. "Can you use one of the guns?"

Barnes leans down slowly and picks up the rifle. "Bullets?"

I nod toward the glove compartment where I stashed them.

He haltingly reloads the gun, his wound and the jarring movement of the truck along the old track making it difficult.

"Now I can," he says eventually, but his face is pale and he's shaking. I don't know how much use he's actually going to be if it comes to a fight.

He sits with the gun held perpendicular to the window for a while, but doesn't speak. I'm not in the mood for small talk either, and concentrate on keeping my hands on the wheel and the truck moving toward freedom. We're most of the way down the track when I see lights in front of us.

I don't need good night vision to see what it is.

It's a group of supers, their spell webs showing up like lights on a Christmas tree as they wait behind their roadblock. I put my foot on the brake and slow the truck to a stop. I don't think they've seen or heard us yet. My stomach tightens and my heart lurches up into my chest. I'd been hoping the two guards I took down were the only people out here.

I should have known better.

"What's happening? Why are we stopping?"

I glance over at Barnes. He can't see the spell web, so it's just inky darkness up ahead.

"They've put up a roadblock on the track. We need to figure out how we're going to get through."

To his credit, he doesn't question me. "How many people?"

I squint ahead, down the hill. "At least five."

"Do they have vehicles?"

I shake my head. "I can't tell. Probably. I can only see the people."

We sit for a moment. One option is to leave the truck and walk out past them through the woods. But I don't know how many other people are in the woods waiting for us, and I don't think Agent Barnes has the energy left to walk, let alone run if we get discovered.

If we just drive through the roadblock, we risk getting shot, and we're going to be a great big moving target for their guns.

"We could split up," I say. "You drive the truck down toward them, going really slow to cause a distraction. I'll go down separately and take a few of them out. Maybe all of them." I glance over at Barnes, not entirely convinced he'd stay conscious long enough to drive the truck to the roadblock.

But he nods, his eyes glittering in the dark. "That's about the best plan we're going to come up with. How long do you want me to wait before following you down?"

I look toward the hill below us. "Ten minutes. Just to make sure I get into the right position."

He nods. "Okay. Let's do this. And fast, before I lose any more blood." He grins, some of his previous charisma returning, despite his gaping gunshot wound. I give him a grim smile, trying to seem reassuring.

Jumping out of the truck, I help him move across to the driver's seat. He straps himself in and nods. "Go. Quickly. We need to get out of here."

I nod and, without another word, head into the woods and disappear into the trees. I run swiftly through the undergrowth, choosing speed over silence at this point. I slow down and walk when I'm closer, until I'm parallel to the roadblock. They're making no attempt to be quiet. Again, they're assuming they have the upper hand; a large automatic machine gun rests on a tripod on the hood of an enormous SUV parked across the road. Another smaller truck sits to one side.

I aim for the two men operating the machine gun first. I don't want to get Agent Barnes any more shot up than he already is. If I can take them out quietly, we have more of a chance.

I use the spell web to see the two men and send out a feeling of being relaxed over the grid. They sit back in their positions and start smiling almost immediately. Moving soundlessly, it takes me no more than a quick pressure onto their necks to knock them out, thanks to Si's training. I'm pulling their bodies quietly to one side when I hear the motor of the truck start up. Not a moment to lose.

Another man comes around the side of the SUV, and I sucker punch him into his stomach, just under the ribs, and then kick his head when he leans over, trying to breathe. He goes down, obviously one of those big guys who relies on never being punched to survive in a fight. He didn't even get a chance to pull out the gun holstered to his side.

The last two men turn when he noisily falls to the ground and their eyes widen when they see me standing in the darkness. I don't have time to get his gun, so I wait.

They glance at each other, and then both rush me at once. They probably expect me to run, but I hold my ground, my hands ready.

I'm relaxed, calm and ready to kick ass.

7

I sidestep the first guy and land a kick to the other guy's side. He goes down heavily, clutching his side.

They're both dressed in the same black shirt and trousers as all the others, with the Earthbound symbol on their shoulders. One guy is taller and has long hair in a ponytail down his back. He's the one lying on the ground wishing I hadn't kicked him.

The other guy is shorter, more solid. He also looks smarter, and I edge warily around him as he considers his next move. By this point, he's realized I've taken out three of the others and I'm not just easy fodder. He glances up the hill to where the truck is rolling slowly down, making as much noise as possible. Agent Barnes is doing an excellent job of distraction. I kick my opponent in the leg, and he stumbles away.

I hear him growl, and then the solid guy charges, and I sidestep, targeting a punch to the neck as he goes by. I miss, but get his shoulder, a bundle of hard muscle, instead. It probably hurt my hand more than his shoulder, and I flick it to alleviate the pain.

I turn quickly, trying to keep both men inside my line of sight. The guy on the ground has pulled himself to his feet, his face a mask of anger. His ponytail is all messed up. He moves forward, aiming a punch toward my face, and I block him, punching his gut and then striking a front kick to his knee. I hear something crack, and he goes down, screaming in pain, holding his knee.

I move back and look around for the other guy, but I'm too late. One thick arm slides around my neck, and he holds me against his chest with the other. The arm around my throat tightens, blocking my airways.

I can't breathe.

Immediately I punch backward with my elbow and he grunts, but doesn't let go. I kick, use my elbows, fingers, and even my head, but he has me securely positioned and he's much stronger than I am. He must be some kind of mountain or stone supernatural.

He contracts his arm even more. I gasp for breath, but it's all blocked off and I'm seeing stars. By this point, I'm grabbing at his arms ineffectually. I try reaching out along the spell web, but it's too late. My mind is already unable to think, unable to use the spell web, unable to fight.

This is it. I'm taken out in my first proper fight, by some goon using brute force. It's a situation I should have known better than to get into. I kick out again, and I know I hurt him, but I can't make him let go.

An explosion echoes through the night, and my captor jerks. For a moment, we both hold still, and then I feel liquid dripping down the side and back of my head. My ears are ringing and I'm having trouble standing up straight.

I recognize the smell before anything else. Blood and gunpowder. He's been shot in the head. My captor falls forward, taking me with him. He lands half on top of me, trapping me under his body. His grip around my throat loosens and I breathe in for the first time in what seems like forever. It hurts like hell, but it's all I can think of at first, getting that next breath into my body.

Eventually, I attempt to push his body off mine. His body is like a damn rock and I'm too weak. I can't budge him. Panic flares. I'm close to the edge, and I open my mouth to scream, but nothing comes out. It's been a tough night, and this is the last straw. I can't handle anymore. All I want to do is curl up and cry. I can feel the tears on my face, mingling with the blood of the dead man lying on top of me.

I hear the truck stop nearby, and a door opens. "Are you coming?" asks Agent Barnes, his voice sounding like it's an effort to even open his mouth, let alone form the words.

"Gimme a sec," I rasp out. Jeff would have said that was a relief, me not being able to talk. He also would have told me to get my lazy butt up off the ground and keep going. I groan, knowing I can't just lie here. Jeff and Si would say it's a waste of all their training. And they'd be right.

"I can't help you," says Agent Barnes.

"I know." I take a deep breath, the air still hurting as it follows my windpipe down to my lungs.

Then I summon every piece of my remaining strength and push at the massive body on top of me. I bend my legs and shove with the soles of my feet, and eventually the dead weight moves.

Once I get him at an angle, it's easier to roll him off. I stand and then kick him, hard. Once, twice, a third time. I can feel a thick liquid dripping down my face and I don't have to touch it to know it's blood and maybe brains. My feet stumble toward the trucks blocking the road. We have to get out of here fast.

Agent Barnes shot him in the head.

I stumble as I think it through. If he'd been off by an inch, he would have killed me. As it is, I feel woozy and unstable. I put one hand to my head, wondering if I've been shot and don't realize it. But there's nothing there except another man's blood and gore.

The only way to deal with it is to block it out and get on with saving ourselves. That's what Jeff would have said.

I climb into the big flashy SUV; the keys are still in the ignition. As I back it off the road, each movement makes my aching muscles scream. I consider taking the SUV, but I know Bertha's capabilities, and I know nothing about this vehicle. It's probably got a tracker on it as well. I shove it in gear, and jump out as it starts rolling toward the forest on one side.

Agent Barnes is waiting in the truck, and I stumble toward him, trying to get my breathing under control and my head in focus. He's managed to get himself across to the passenger seat, and I head around to the driver's side. By the time I climb into the cab, I'm calmer, and I re-start the engine.

"Thanks," I say. "I would have died if you hadn't taken that shot." I want to shout at him, tell him my ears are still ringing. But I don't.

He nods, saying nothing.

We go through the roadblock and continue down the old track. Turning onto the highway, I drive automatically, trying to put as much distance between us and the Earth-bound as I can. Beside me, Agent Barnes slumps in his seat, the seatbelt the only thing holding him up.

He needs medical attention, and I can't give it to him. Not properly. I can't take him to a hospital. He's become a casualty in the hidden war between myself and the Earthbound.

There's only one option that I can think of, but it means driving south for several hours. I shake my arms out. I don't know if I can stay awake that long, but I'm going to try.

8

The first couple of hours are uneventful. As the sun is rising in the distance, I turn on Bertha's radio, trying to keep myself awake.

The news comes on at the top of the hour.

"This just in: an emergency lockdown is in place around the town of Keepsake and the Whitlow Forest area. Civilians are asked to stay away while emergency personnel hunt for a dangerous escaped convict. Described as a slight part-Asian woman with long dark hair, Mei Walker is considered to be armed and dangerous. She's driving an old blue pickup truck, registration 47C 72N2. Do not approach. I repeat, do not approach, she is armed and dangerous."

My hands shake on the steering wheel and I glance around me on the highway. The morning sunrise brightens the landscape even as I watch. The truck is visible to everyone with two eyes and a radio to listen to. Anyone could call in my whereabouts to the Earthbound now, even humans.

Previously, I only had to worry about supernaturals

phoning me in for the bounty; but now, apparently, the Earthbound are going wider.

They're more desperate.

It's getting closer to my twentieth birthday.

I don't even know precisely what is going to happen when I turn twenty, or why the Earthbound feel so sure I'm going to harm the spell web. It's like I'm being blamed for a crime I didn't commit. The knowledge burns at my insides.

If I knew more, perhaps I could make better decisions. This is the one thing I've fought consistently with Si and Jeff over. I'm convinced they've always known who and what I am, but they chose not to tell me.

It's hard not to feel some satisfaction that I was right. This wouldn't be such a mess now if they'd just told me. I'd have some idea where to go, what to do. I don't have them here to look after me anymore, and the secrets they kept have gone with them.

I slam the steering wheel with the palm of one hand.

What the hell am I going to do? I can't drive another hour in this damn pickup truck if there's a national bulletin out on it. And Agent Barnes is breathing shallowly beside me; he's not going to survive much longer.

I bite my lip, thinking hard. Who else could I go to, who's close? I drive past the Giant Chicken advertising a BBQ restaurant at the Ramsgate turnoff, and a name pops into my mind.

Rupert.

I shake my head and immediately decide against it. He hates me. He'll hate me more when he discovers Jeff is dead. I tap my finger on the steering wheel, trying to think of an alternative.

But eventually I sigh. Rupert might just be the only person who can keep Agent Barnes alive. He might even have another vehicle I can use. I need to get over the fact that he hates me and do what's best for Agent Barnes. I change lanes and get off at the next exit. Then I get back onto the highway and drive to the Giant Chicken motorway sign.

Ramsgate is a strange and intriguing town.

It's full of supernaturals, so we usually avoid it, but I've been once or twice to visit. Rupert's an old friend of Jeff's, they go back a long way, and there's a bit of life-saving thrown in there somewhere. I don't know who saved whom, but it hardly matters at this point.

I'm not sure how he's going to take Jeff's death. Other than to be pissed at me. He blames me whenever they have a fight. My knuckles turn white as my fingers tighten on the steering wheel. I'm not sure I'm going to be able to tell him.

I drive through the small town, trying to act casual and not notice how everyone is staring at my truck. How many people actually listen to the radio these days? Surely not that many.

Rupert's place is on the other side of town, an old run-down farm that looks almost deserted. He's a druid, born and raised in Ireland by a mysterious society that trained him in all the healing arts. He could fix Agent Barnes with one arm tied behind his back, if he agrees.

Jeff always refused to tell me what caused Rupert to land here, miles from home, bitter and angry at the world, but I'm pretty sure it was bad. He now wastes most of his time looking for gold in the nearby mountains. He's always said the farm is a front for his gold business.

I park Bertha outside the old metal gate and give Agent Barnes a shake on the arm. He groggily opens his eyes, and I manage to carry him through the gate and down the short track to Rupert's house. It looks deserted, almost a ruin, but I know better than to be fooled.

"Rupert! Come out. I need your help," I yell, my voice low and rusty. As I stand on the semi-rotten deck, a face peeks out one of the dirty windows. "I saw you! Open the door, or I'm going to break it down." I swallow hard over the pain in my throat from my near-death experience.

I wouldn't speak like this to just anyone, but Rupert and I have a history of hating each other. He's also got a thick skin, so normal talk won't get through to him. You've really got to lay on the charm.

Nothing else moves in the house for a full minute. I clear my throat. "Okay then. I'm gonna do it. Your damn door is coming down." I lift my foot for a kick, Agent Barnes still dangling off my side.

The door opens, and a tall, thin, red-haired shaggy-looking man stands in the frame. He's wearing jeans and a dirty white t-shirt. "What the hell are you doing here? Your name and face are all over the human media. You're gonna lead them all to me." His face is red and puffy, and he's holding a tissue in one hand.

"Have you been crying?" I ask, pushing my way past him into the dark and damp hallway.

"Is it true? Jeff's dead?"

I lay Barnes on the sofa and turn to Rupert. Tears swim in my eyes, and I can only bring myself to nod. I swallow hard despite the pain it causes my throat.

"Si too?"

Another nod.

"What the hell happened?"

I gesture to Barnes. "He led them to us. I don't think he meant to, but he had a tracking spell inserted under his subconscious. Jeff thought he'd been sent by someone trustworthy." I shrug.

"You're going to lead them to me." It's not a question.

"I need you to heal him. I'll leave as soon as it's done." I look at Rupert, tears swimming in my eyes. "You can say I forced you to do it at gunpoint."

He shakes his head. "No. You have to leave. You've set me up for a world of trouble as it is, coming here like this."

"You have to," I say, trying to keep my voice calm.

"The Earthbound will ask me questions. Questions I can't answer." Rupert's face is a mask of anguish now. "Jeff was my friend, a good friend. He saved me more than once. But he's dead, like I always said he would be, because of you."

My knees go weak and I only just manage to hold myself up. He's not saying anything that's not true. "This isn't about me. This is about an agent who is caught up in something he didn't understand. Don't let him die." I take a step toward Rupert, and I see the fear flash in his eyes.

I stop. He's afraid of me? "Just heal him quickly, and we'll be on our way."

"You'll need more than a quick healing from me to save him."

"Then hurry up and do what you can!" My voice rises, cracking in the middle, and I feel the anger pulling at me. Si and Jeff's deaths have me closer to the edge than I've ever been in my life. I don't need this kind of aggravation.

Rupert looks at me for a second, indecision in his eyes. The fear has been buried again, and I'm relieved. I don't like to think I scare people and that perhaps the Earthbound are right about me.

Rupert walks over to Agent Barnes and rolls him onto his back. He stares down at him, as if memorizing his face.

"Hurry up," I say. "If you don't get on with it, you're going to be caught up in the middle of something you might not survive either."

Rupert scowls at me, but does as I say. "Don't think I'm going to heal you too," he mutters as he places his hands on the agent's head. I don't care, as long as he makes Agent Barnes better. I'm not going to have another death hanging around my neck if I can help it.

Rupert closes his eyes and starts chanting a spell under his breath. I know it's possible to do the magic without the words, so I figure he's just doing it for effect. Before long, the wispy cloud-like particles of a healing spell surround the agent. It's strongest around his bullet wound and is almost like a living thing, the way it moves forward and backward, trying to find an entrance that will allow it to enter.

It sinks slowly into his body, and soon Rupert starts shaking from the effort.

This is no more than I expected. Whenever Si did this kind of healing, it took a massive amount out of him, and I always had a feeling he was much stronger than he let on. Rupert the stupid druid is probably going to have to take to his bed for a week after this.

I hope he has a good hideaway, because the Earthbound will close in on us pretty quickly given the looks we got coming into town.

At first, I stand at the entrance to the living room, glaring at Rupert, making sure he doesn't try anything. But the feeling of something dripping down my neck reminds me I have blood all over me. The bathroom is just down the hall, and I run my head under the shower, trying to get the worst of it out. My hair and face are soaked, but I feel better. Then I notice a large blood stain on the shoulder of my shirt. It's too much, I can't leave it there. I take off my top and wash it under the tap, then wring it out.

I check all the cupboards and find a hair dryer, drying the top as much as I can. Luckily, it's black, so it's hard to see the damp bits. Then I head back out into the living room to check on the druid. He's standing over Barnes in exactly the same stance as when I left.

I sigh and resume my vigil, watching the healing process.

When the doorbell rings, I jump. Rupert doesn't acknowledge he's heard anything, so, heart pounding, I creep over to the door and look through the peephole. Three people wait on the doorstep. I know two of them, but even then I hesitate. Surely I shouldn't open the door?

"We know you're in there, Mei. You may as well open the door. We're not going to turn you in," says a tall willowy woman with long blonde hair and too much makeup.

Melinda is a water supernatural like me, but she's been on land so long, she's forgotten how to swim. She gave it all up for the man standing next to her.

Herman is handsome, I'll give him that. He's tall, dark eyed, and his smile could knock people out. And often does. He's got some kind of persuasion ability and can hypnotize humans, tricking them into doing whatever he wants.

His powers are hit and miss with supernaturals.

More of Jeff's buddies, people he's met over the years. Mostly he's saved them from being captured or put down by the SIG. It was part of his problem as a younger agent, and why he was assigned to me.

I open the door, and they immediately crowd into the hallway. Melinda crushes me into an overly tight hug, and I squirm, trying to back away. She doesn't let go, and despite my strength, I'm pretty much trapped until she decides to stop.

"Is it true? Did the Earthbound kill Jeff and Si?" Her voice is breathy and seductive.

I nod.

She turns to the third person. "I told you. They can't be trusted."

He's a short, unassuming, middle-aged man, with brown hair, and glasses over his brown eyes. He looks ordinary, and immediately I'm suspicious. Si used to look like that a lot. "You're a chameleon," I say.

He nods. "I knew Si and the other Protectors who were tasked with looking after you."

My heart jumps into my throat, and I wonder what he thinks. All five of my Protectors are now dead because of me. I can only stare at him.

He stares back for a moment, and then sighs. "Si always spoke well of you. He said you were worth it. I hope he's right."

I can only shake my head. "No one is worth their deaths," I say, and I mean it. "What are you doing here? You need to keep away from me. The Earthbound are stepping up their searches."

Melinda nods. "They got a whiff of you when they killed Si and Jeff, and now they're desperate to have you. Everyone knows it, but not everyone is on their side." She looks conspiratorially left and right. "There are some people who believe that the Earthbound have overstepped their bounds. That we no longer need the spell web, but they're holding it in place just to keep their power."

I blink. It's the same argument Jeff had with Agent Barnes. "And you think I'm going to be able to help with that?" I feel the spell web coating me like a warm blanket and shudder at the thought of it disappearing.

"The Earthbound certainly do. That's why they're chasing you. At least that's what Jeff thought."

I know Jeff's thoughts on the spell web. That, at least, he wasn't shy about telling me. I just didn't agree with him. "He didn't know that for certain. I don't think anyone knows why the Earthbound are so determined to find me."

"Your father knows." The quiet words are spoken from the room behind us. Agent Barnes is awake.

Everyone turns to look at the agent, who is now sitting up. He still looks pale, but his eyes are clear and focused. Rupert is sitting on a chair nearby, his eyes closed, his face haggard, and his hands hanging limply at each side.

"My father?" I say cautiously.

"It's the only possible conclusion. Of course he knows who and what you are."

Melinda nods next to me. "I've always thought that as well."

I flick my gaze to her, only to find her staring at me like I'm an insect under the microscope. "If my father knows, why didn't Jeff know?"

"But that's the point. I think Jeff *did* know. He just didn't tell *you*," says Agent Barnes.

Even though it's what I've always thought, the hurt twists through my stomach.

9

I shake my head. "It doesn't matter now—"

I'm interrupted by the sound of several helicopters flying overhead. "They're here," I whisper. It's faster than I was expecting.

Melinda nods. "That's what we came to tell you. Old man Pinkerton rang the hotline number and gave a false direction, thinking he was helping you. Didn't realize they'd be able to trace his call. He's drawn them here."

"Then we have to go," I say, already striding over to Agent Barnes, pulling him to his feet. "They were heading to the north side of town. We'll take the old dirt road and head south."

"Your pickup truck is on every radio and television station around here," says Herman. "You're being pegged as a dangerous criminal to the humans. You can't go in that vehicle."

"Then how?"

"There's an old walking track," says the chameleon. "It takes you out onto the other side of the mountain. They won't look for you there. At least not yet. I can take you, but you have to come now. Melinda and Herman will help Rupert cover your tracks here. We must hurry." His spell web glows brightly for a moment.

"What do we do after getting to the other side?" I'm trying to figure out our next move. The safe house is still a long way away.

"There's a track that leads down into the next ridge. There's an old hut there you can stay at for the night, and an old jeep you can take. You'll need to move on quickly." The chameleon watches me closely, waiting for me to agree.

I hesitate. But common sense wins out. They're right. We'd never make it anywhere in Bertha. "Okay." I nod. We'll have to figure out the next move once we're out of this town.

I turn to look at Agent Barnes. He's is standing, steadier than he's been since he was shot.

"How do you feel?" I ask.

"Well enough."

"If you want to stay here, I'll understand. You're hit." The thought of being alone turns me cold all over. But he barely knows me. Why should he risk his life for me?

"I was assigned to protect you. I'm not going anywhere." He gives me his intense stare, his face serious.

I can't help my small relieved grin.

"Great job you're doing of that so far." Melinda's tone is sharp.

He ignores her. "We need to hurry. Let's go." He strides to the front door and puts one hand out to open it.

"Not that door," the chameleon snaps. He leads the way toward the kitchen.

I turn quickly to Melinda and Herman. "You'll look after Rupert?" I say. He doesn't deserve to be in the firing line because of me.

"We'll sort it out. He'll be fine. Just go." Melinda pushes

me toward the door that the others have already exited through.

We follow the chameleon up a path through the woods behind Rupert's house.

"Do you have a way to contact your father?" Agent Barnes asks in an undertone beside me.

I shake my head, glancing up ahead at the chameleon. "No phone, no way to contact him. I only know that SIG headquarters are in New York and he's based there when he's in the country."

Agent Barnes nods as if he'd figured as much. "I think we need to get to your father. We should head toward New York."

"There's a safe house near here—"

He shakes his head quickly. "We need to get to your father as soon as we can, so he can sort this mess out. He's the only one who knows the whole story. You and me, we don't know what the hell's going on here, right?"

I reluctantly nod. It's what I've been saying to myself.

"Then we need to go to the one person who can tell us."

"Okay." He's right. It's our best option.

We climb in silence for a while, until I realize Melinda never officially introduced us to the chameleon. I move up beside him. "What's your name?" I ask.

"Ben." His tone is short, not encouraging chitchat. That's fine with me. We climb higher and higher through the woods in silence, none of us inclined to talk.

I can hear Agent Barnes puffing behind me, but he doesn't utter a word of complaint. He looks fit, and I know they work the cadets at the academy hard, so I don't imagine he's used to being out of breath on a simple walk like this. His wound isn't completely healed though, and he's going to suffer if we do much more physical activity.

"How much further?" I ask Ben.

"Not far," he mutters. "Just up ahead."

I haven't heard or seen any more of the helicopters that flew over. I hope, for Old Man Pinkerton's sake, that they dismissed his call as the ramblings of an old man.

We run out of trees for protection, and now we're climbing over large rocks, with a scattering of stones. I slide over the small pebbles, falling onto one knee, and blood appears over the scrape.

But I just pull myself to my feet again and carry on. My arms are aching from hauling myself up over the boulders, and the sun is hot on my back.

Eventually Ben calls a halt. I help pull Agent Barnes up over the last rock and look around. We're all standing on a small flat section of the mountain, and in the distance I can see a tall, narrow cave opening in the rock. I can't see more than a couple of feet past the entrance.

"This is where I'll leave you. Just go through here and it will lead you to the other side. Then head down the track and you should find the hut where I've got the car stashed. You can take that." He hands me a set of keys.

I nod. "Thank you for your help. I appreciate it."

Something flashes in his eyes, and for the thousandth time I wish I could read people like Jeff. It feels like he's annoyed at me for some reason. "Did you know Si well?" I ask. Perhaps he blames me for his death, the way Rupert does for Jeff.

Ben shakes his head. "No. I knew Lee, one of your other protectors far better." He pauses. "He was my brother."

At the mention of Lee's name, I see myself being bounced on Lee's knee, and of him showing me how to swim in the Mississippi river. I smile warmly. "Lee was a wonderful person," I say.

Ben nods solemnly. "Yes, he was." He turns away, already starting to climb downward. "I wish you luck on your journey. You'll need it."

I frown at Agent Barnes who shrugs. "He's right. We *will* need luck to survive this."

The dark cave looms beside us. It's more a crack in the rock than a proper cave opening. I try to peer inside, but can't see a thing. "You ready for this, Agent Barnes?" I say.

"Call me Seth," he says softly. "Once you've saved my life, you get to use my first name." He's staring at me, his hazel eyes hooded.

"Seth, then," I say. I take a breath. "Let's get going."

The first few steps into the cave don't seem so bad. The light is still behind us, and my eyes acclimatize quickly to the darkness. But after a few minutes, the light from the opening narrows and disappears. I can see a little, probably more than Seth, but the further we go, the more it seems to crowd in. The ceiling pushes down on me, and it's like I'm trapped in a dark, damp, ever-decreasing cell. No windows or doors, and no way out. I start gasping for air, and my head feels woozy.

"Mei. Calm down." Hands grasp my arms from behind, and Seth turns me around, leaving his hands on my shoulders. He moves so his head is level with mine and looks me in the eye. "Take slow breaths."

I try to do what he says, but all I can manage are shallow inhalations. "I... don't... know what's... the matter." I've never had a problem with caves before. I'm not used to being so lame.

"You're having a panic attack. It's okay. We're okay." He rubs his thumbs over the place where my shoulders meet my neck, and I nod, still trying to get myself back in control.

I don't understand what's happening.

As I concentrate on breathing in, I catch the scent of gunpowder and pine, mixed with an undertone of blood. My gaze flicks up to Seth; his hazel eyes are watching me like a hawk's. I inhale again. He's so close, his unique scent fills my senses; suddenly all I can think about is leaning forward into his body. My breath hitches, and I swallow hard. The urge is unlike anything I've ever experienced before.

I close my eyes and try to block it out—block him out.

I need to get myself under control and get out of here. I focus on my breathing, and soon I'm back to normal. Seth straightens up and moves away.

"I've never... felt like that before," I say. My brain is mixed up and I don't know whether I mean the panicked breathing or the reaction to his scent.

Luckily, Seth doesn't know about the second option.

"It could have been a delayed reaction to what you went through against the Earthbound," he says. "That guy had his arms pretty tight around your neck. You're going to have bruises."

I wince and put one hand up to my neck. It's tender and sore. Seth is probably right.

"Thank you," I whisper. And I really mean it.

He doesn't say anything for a moment. "We have to keep going."

Taking another deep breath, I step forward. I miss the warmth from Seth's hands. Briefly, I consider asking to hold his hand, but I manage to keep silent. I'm not comfortable showing that level of weakness to him. Bad enough that he saw me lose control just now.

I'm back in command, and I need to stay that way.

It seems like forever, but it's probably no more than half an hour before we see a light up ahead in the tunnel. It becomes bigger and bigger until we're only yards away from the opening. I'm about to step out into the open air, ready to take a deep breath of sweet fresh oxygen, when Seth grabs my arm. "Did you hear that?" he whispers, holding me next to him. His muscled arm brushes my shoulder.

"Hear what?"

"I think there's someone out there," he says. "Stay here. I'll check first." Seth goes down low and creeps to the edge of the cave entrance. He peers around, and then pulls back quickly.

"What is it?" I whisper. I really didn't hear whatever it is he's heard. He might have just saved us.

"You better come have a look for yourself," he says, his voice grim.

I peer around the edge of the rock; on the grassy valley below us are three helicopters. Supernatural guards are spewed out across the valley, their spell webs clear and strong. I don't know how I could have missed them. Most are waiting around the cave, their guns trained on the entrance. If they've seen us, they're not letting on.

"Holy shit," I say. "We better turn around." Even as I say it, I hear footsteps echoing in the tunnel behind us. "They're back there as well, aren't they?"

"I think so. It would make sense." He glances at me, his hazel eyes bright. "It appears your friends aren't as friendly as you thought."

Shaking my head, I think it through. The others might have their faults, but I can't believe they'd turn us in. "It must have been the chameleon, Ben."

"Why?"

I pause, and let out a small sigh. "He thinks I caused his brother's death." Of course he does. I don't know why it didn't occur to me before.

"Did you?"

"In the same way I cause everyone's deaths," I say, my voice cracking. "Because they're protecting me."

"Then it's not your fault. They chose to protect you."

A sudden anger washes over me. "They're doing it for nothing, you know. I'm just an ordinary girl."

Seth's eyebrows rise, but he doesn't say anything.

I let out a frustrated breath. "For a supernatural, I mean. There are any number of supers out there who have the same kind of magic as me. It's nothing that should make the Earthbound hunt me down for my entire life. I'm not worth it." Tears well in my eyes, and I swipe them away with the back of one hand.

"That's quite a pity party you've got going on there," Seth drawls.

I glare at him, but something inside me lightens. For a second, he sounds a bit like Jeff.

"It's not you killing them. It's the Earthbound. And if they believe it's okay to attack and kill someone like you, then I think Melinda might be right. Perhaps they *have* overstepped their bounds."

I look back around the edge of the rock. There are at least twenty men out there, all armed and dangerous. They look much more intimidating than the men I saw at Si's house. The sound of jogging boots on the cave floor is louder now too, as the men behind us jog closer to our position. It's sending vibrations along the rock and up through my arms. We're surrounded. "What are we going to do?" I ask.

"Do you want to get out of this?"

I nod. "Of course I do."

"Then we fight."

"And how the hell do we do that?" I'm used to bad odds;

Jeff and Si made me defend myself against all sorts of nasty creatures, including themselves. But we're trapped.

"The men behind us are stuck inside as well. They can only go one man at a time through a narrow pass. I have a few rounds left in my gun; I can hold off the ones behind us. I need you to figure out some way to get us to the helicopters."

"Can you fly a helicopter?"

"I've had some training."

I don't trust the look in his eyes. "But—"

"COME OUT NOW, AND WE'LL LET THE SIG AGENT GO," a voice calls out through a megaphone. I lean back around the edge of the rock. They're all looking straight at us.

This is it. We're screwed.

10

Nothing happens for a few minutes after that. The man on the loud speaker and another man are conferring. I can almost hear it now. *You can't promise that. We're not authorized to let him go*, says the first guy. *Don't worry, I'm not going to let him go,* says the second guy. *I'm just telling her that so she'll give herself up.*

"Can you do anything that might help us here?" Seth asks.

I glance back at him. "I can manipulate water. Maybe there's something out there that will help." I look out at the valley. There must be a stream for it to be so fertile. But I can't sense it.

I can use the spell web. That's the other thing I can do, but I'm not telling Seth that.

Looking out along the spell web, I send a tendril of thought along its lines, to see if I can find anything useful. Every single one of the men is supernatural. Not just that, but I realize the glow of the spell web over their bodies is much brighter than normal. Like, almost too bright to look at. I frown. Something strange is going on.

Squinting, I try to see what it is. I push a bit of my magic out over the spell web, and as soon as it touches the first supernatural guard, the electric shock of an energy blast zings back to me like lightning along the web. I swear, and shake my head as the pain reverberates inside my brain. I've never felt anything like it.

"Are you okay?" Seth asks.

"Yeah." I don't know how to explain without giving away my secret, so I don't.

Peering out at the guards again, I try to figure out what this means. Somehow their magic has been amped up through the spell web and they're using it as a weapon. What else can they do when they're like this? The thought makes me shiver. As if the Earthbound weren't powerful enough.

Then another thought occurs to me and I frown. Could the Earthbound soldiers be sucking more energy than they're supposed to from the spell web to amp up their own magic?

That would definitely be overstepping the bounds. It would send the supernatural community into turmoil. Using a portion of our powers to maintain the spell web is seen as a necessary evil; if it turns out they're taking advantage of it, supers everywhere would bay for the blood of the Earthbound.

Unfortunately, that doesn't help us right now. I don't know how to fight this many trained guards. We're probably going to die here without letting this particular secret out.

Glancing at Seth, I try to think. I refuse to let us die because of me. "They've all got extra power from the spell web. They're too strong," I say.

Seth's face hardens. "Then we just have to figure something else out. We need to turn this situation on its head, do something they wouldn't expect. I think we should go back through the tunnels and take on the men following us. We'll have better odds."

Turn this situation in its head? My brain snags on his words. It sounds like something Jeff would say. Again.

If they're taking power from the spell web, they would have to be more connected to it than most supernaturals. I've been manipulating the spell web for a long time now; I have a few tricks up my sleeve. "I... I think I'm going to try something else first," I say. "I might just be able to get us out of this, but I'm not sure it's going to work. So..."

"Be ready for anything?"

"Yes. That." I give him a half smile. If I can manipulate the direction of the lightning and push the electricity back onto the guards, their stronger connection might actually mean they'll be knocked out. It sounds crazy, but crazy is all I have to work with right now.

Looking down at the spell web as it surrounds me, I concentrate on becoming part of it, of melding my power into its steady heartbeat. It's like becoming part of nature, of everything around us. I focus on building up an excess of energy, creating a layer of magic strong enough to block the electricity and knock it back into the guards. It's our only hope of getting anywhere near the helicopter.

Soon I feel the sizzling magic spitting and hissing inside me. "Wish me luck," I say.

"Luck."

I push it out in one giant burst, aiming along all angles of the spell web. Time seems to stand still, and I hold my breath, waiting to see what happens. The lines light up so bright I almost can't see them. A tidal wave of power is hurtling along the grids. I'm half-expecting the energy to come back and hit me like a ton of bricks.

The energy hits the first man. He groans, then collapses. One after the other in quick succession, like pins at a bowling alley, the men waiting to kill us are knocked out.

I'm still for a moment, kind of surprised. Then I let out a breath.

Seth stands up. "It worked. Let's go." He grabs my hand and we race across the field to the helicopter. He doesn't seem to realize that what I've just done is outside of what a supernatural should be able to do.

My heart is pumping hard, and I'm watching the men, waiting for one of them to sit up and hold a gun on us, yelling, "Fooled you!"

Not one of them moves.

"What did you do to them?" Seth glances around as we run.

"I electrocuted them a little bit. They're not dead." *I think.* I cross the fingers on my other hand.

We reach the helicopter, and I'm about to pull open the door, when a figure steps around the side. He's of medium height, stocky, with piercing brown eyes and tightly trimmed grey hair. He holds himself like he knows how to fight, and I can tell he'd be a difficult opponent if it came to that. "Stop right there," he says. He's aiming a nasty-looking handgun at my heart.

I go automatically into a fighting stance. Beside me, I feel Seth tense up.

"There's no point fighting. This gun will win out every time."

I can see Si inside my mind, shaking his head. Not *every* time.

I run through all the techniques Si has taught me to take out someone with a gun. But I don't say a word. I need to get a handle on who this man is and why he's after me. He seems different, maybe someone higher up the food chain. He might actually know something about me and why the Earthbound are so desperate to kill me.

I peer at him closely. His spell web is glowing, but not with the artificial brightness of the other men. That's how he survived being knocked out. He wasn't connected to it like they were. "You're leading this operation," I say. It's not a question.

He nods once. "My name is Vincent. I'm curious to know how you managed to knock out all my men." He glances over at the field full of unconscious guards. "And more importantly, how long it will be before they're mobile again?"

"I don't know. A while."

"Then I have no choice." His finger tightens on the trigger of his gun, and I move to one side, but it's too late. A tiny dart enters the skin on my neck. He shoots Seth with another dart, and seconds later, Seth collapses. I take a couple of steps toward Vincent before my concrete-filled legs harden. I glance down in surprise, and then the ground hurtles toward me.

Then nothing.

11

I slowly emerge from a deep fog. At first I can't remember anything, my brain keeps circling around and around. Then I feel pain, and I don't know why. I don't open my eyes, it takes too much energy.

I'm lying on my side, and I try to move my arms, but can't. Rope scratches against my wrists. They're tied tight to each other. My ankles hurt; they're probably tied up as well.

I'm in a moving vehicle, and every time we go over a bump, my shoulder slams into something hard and metal. My head is pounding like I've been hit over the head with a hammer. Maybe several hammers. Opening my eyes a tiny bit reveals that I'm in total darkness.

I open my eyes wide and look around. Where the hell am I? And how did I get here? Why didn't he just kill me?

It feels like a van, and we're going over a particularly bumpy road with no suspension and a driver who feels the need for speed. He goes over a big bump and I get a bit of air time, landing with a thump. I groan in pain.

"She's coming round," says a worried voice from behind me.

"Can't be. The boss said she'd be out for the count until we got there."

"She made a noise. Didn't you hear?"

Clothes rustle, and I imagine an unconcerned shrug.

So, I have two guards in back with me. I squint toward the front of the van. I can't see through the gap to how many guards might be in the front. At least one more driving.

My next concern is Seth. Is he here with me?

At the next big bump, I try to turn myself around slightly so I'm facing a little more into the middle of the van. I keep my eyes closed for a minute afterward, trying to breathe shallowly and slowly and hold myself limp.

"She's moved around. Did you see that? She wasn't looking that way before."

"You're an idiot. She's dead to the world. That last bump was a big 'un, that's all."

"But—"

"I'm gonna tell the boss you're not up to these kind of jobs, if you keep whining."

The threat of what would happen to the whiner was enough. Is Vincent the boss? Or do I have some new person to contend with? Whoever it is, he isn't someone they want to mess with.

I open my eyes a sliver and see another lump nearby. Seth. I relax slightly. They've brought him with us, so at least he's considered important enough to keep alive. I'm not entirely certain why we *are* still alive, but I'm not going to argue about it.

My hands are behind my back, and hopefully not visible to my guards, so I start trying to wriggle them free. It's hard work, because my movements have to be so small. Every time we go over a bump I do a big pull on the rope, and after a while, the knots start to loosen. Not enough to get my hands out, though.

Across from me, Seth groans.

"Now he's awake. I told you!" The whiner is down on his knees next to me in a heartbeat, opening my eyes with a stubby finger. I fight to stay limp, but the grubby little bastard pokes his fingers on my eye. I can't do it any longer. I move my head and bite his finger, letting go as I flick my legs up and around, kicking his head. He's blown back across the van and hits the side.

"Ha-ha. I win the bet." A nasty troll-like face comes to crouch down next to me, holding a Taser. Before I can move away, he shoves it into my neck. I jerk stiff, and then shake uncontrollably while the electric currents storm through my body.

"You try anything funny, and I'll stick more into you." He stops the flow of electricity to my neck, and reaches out with the other hand and grasps my breast painfully. He rubs his hand around a few times, grinning down at me the whole time.

I stare stonily back.

He laughs and goes back to sit on the side, leaving the Taser pins stuck into my neck. I shudder as the remains of the electricity zings through my body, making my legs shake and my head pound.

I don't know how much time has passed when the van slams to a halt. I slide along the metal floor and slam into the front.

"Come on. Get up you two. I know you're both awake." He sniggers and sends a zap of electricity into me through the Taser.

I groan, unable to force myself to move. I feel rather than see Seth trying to sit up.

"You're going to have to undo my legs if you expect me to walk anywhere," he says calmly.

I wish I could be so calm.

"Boss said no. So I guess we'll be carrying you."

I start to struggle at the idea of either of these two putting their hands on me again. My brain is a little messed up from the electricity from the Taser.

"I want the little one," says the whiner. "I'm too small to carry the big guy."

There's a moment of silence while the bastard with the Taser assesses the situation. "Fine. Take the Taser. We'll have our chance with her later anyway. Once the boss is finished with her." He leers down at me and stomps over to Seth, picking him up in one go and slamming him over his shoulder. Seth's grunt is enough to tell me it was painful.

The whiner leans down and picks me up cautiously. "Don't try anything," he says, and he lifts me over his shoulder. I look down at his dirty ass, and wish I had the balls to bite him on it.

But I've been Tasered one too many times since awakening in the van, and my head doesn't feel right anymore. I can't do anything but let him take me where he's going to take me. I close my eyes and let my body hang down, trying not to imagine what might happen later when the other guy gets his way.

It seems like forever before he pulls me from his shoulder and drops me to the ground, but it can't be more than a couple of minutes. Cold tiles soothe my battered body, and I lay my face against the smooth coolness.

"What have you done to her?" The voice is soft, but I can feel the vibrations of anger even without opening my eyes. It seems familiar, but I can't place it at first.

"We brought her to you. As requested, boss," the bigger guy says smugly.

"I didn't tell you to beat her," says the voice again. "Or Taser her." It's Vincent.

"She woke up, tried to make trouble..." the whiner says.

"Two grown men can't take care of a little girl without beating her? What kind of men do I employ?"

I open my eyes, interested in watching their faces. The big guy's assertion that they'll get me later seems to have been nothing more than wishful thinking. "I didn't..." I clear my croaky throat. "I didn't do anything," I manage to get out.

"You knocked me across the van," squeaks the whiner.

"You opened my eyes and poked your dirty finger on my eyeball," I say. "What the hell else was I supposed to do?"

"A normal person might have asked me to stop!"

"A normal person wouldn't have done that in the first place," I shoot back.

"Enough! You two, report to your section leader. You will be demoted for the next full quarter and receive deducted pay. Next time, treat my guests properly."

"Yes, boss," they mutter in unison, and shuffle out of the room.

Vincent nods at someone outside of my view, and I'm grasped by two sets of hands who pull me up to standing. The ropes are cut, and I'm suddenly free. I stumble and almost fall as the blood flows back into my limbs. Only the hands of my unknown helpers keep me from falling.

"Get her a seat. And the SIG agent."

I glance over at Seth; he's having similar problems. A chair is gently forced under my knees, and I flop down, unconcerned about looking elegant—or even upright.

"I apologize for their behavior. I thought they could be

trusted on this one small job. Clearly I was wrong. Next time I will ensure I use more trusted members of staff."

I blink warily up at him. He's standing in the middle of a large room. Light from enormous skylights overhead makes the room glow. There are pictures painted around the room depicting men and women in brave poses, usually standing over the dead bodies of dragons. It can only be the headquarters of the Earthbound.

"Why are we here?" I ask, my voice low and throaty. I clear my throat again. "Why didn't you just kill us?"

"For the same reason I have been searching for you for so long, my dear." He starts to pace, rubbing his hands together like he's about to open a particularly good present on Christmas morning.

I frown. "And that would be?"

He stops and walks back to where Seth and I are sitting. He bends over, so his eyes are level with mine, and gazes at me. "Can it be that you truly don't know?"

"Don't know what?" I'm tired of his cryptic remarks.

He smiles and stands up straight. "I didn't know you would be so clueless. I assumed they would have told you." He turns and walks away, his finger tapping his chin, as if considering.

"Just tell me what the hell you're talking about!" I growl out. I'm tempted to stamp my feet at him.

Vincent turns back to me, dramatically swirling his coat. I wonder how many hours he had to practice in front of the mirror to achieve that. "You are very special, Mei. You're the last of your kind, you see. There is no one else like you."

"Water magic is a dime a dozen. I'm not special."

His eyes light up. "You don't have water magic, my dear. You *are* water magic. You are the last of the dragons."

12

"You mean all this time you've been trying to kill me and the people I love, because you thought I was a dragon?" I whisper. I open my mouth and let out a loud laugh. I can't help it. It's either that or cry.

I keep laughing, the sound becoming hysterical, until I lean over and vomit onto the floor in front of me.

"That's not the reaction I was expecting." Vincent gestures to someone behind me. "Clean it up."

Minions appear from nowhere, and within minutes, it's as if the vomit was never there. Except I can still taste the bitterness of bile on my tongue.

It's all so absurd, I can't begin to comprehend the totality of his mistake and what it's cost me. Faces flash in my head: Si and Jeff, Lee and the other Protectors, my mother—she's a vague blurry shape. All of them dead for no reason.

"I don't *think* you're a dragon. I know it. Your mother was a dragon and she passed it down the line to you."

I shake my head, my hair swishing angrily. "It's not true. Don't you think I'd know if I was a dragon?"

"I don't know what you've been told, but it's clearly not

the truth." Vincent walks closer to me, peering at my face like I'm a strange and unusual bug he's found. "You really didn't know, did you?"

My body feels heavy and limp, and I have a pounding headache. I can't deal with a lunatic right now. "What are you going to do with me? Why did you bring me here?" I can barely keep my eyes open, and he's looking blurry. "If I'm a dragon, why didn't you just kill me?"

"I never wanted you dead, my dear; at least not for the last few years. That's not the reason I wanted to find you," says Vincent.

My eyes widen and blood rushes back into my head. "Of course it is! It's all you've been trying to do since I was born."

Vincent shakes his head. "I will admit I wasn't too bothered about the lives of your Protectors or the interfering SIG agents." He pauses to glance at Seth. "But I haven't been trying to kill you for a while now. Not since I realized you could be the savior of our world."

My fuzzy brain can't understand what he's telling me. It's so different to what I've grown up knowing. I shake my head, trying to clear it.

Vincent snaps his fingers. "Amos. Take two guards and show our guests to their rooms." Another figure appears at his side, a younger version of Vincent.

"Yes, father." Vincent's son seems baby-faced and naïve standing next to his father, but I'm fairly sure he's older than me, at least in his early twenties. He's got kind brown eyes and shaggy black hair that curls against his collar.

Vincent turns to me. "I will answer the rest of your questions in due course. But for now, I can see you are tired. Make yourself at home. Bathe. Make use of a change of clothing. Sleep." He turns away to talk to an older man standing on the sidelines.

I look at the guards standing next to me, and then past them to Seth. His guards have pulled him to his feet. It's not a request.

"If you will follow me," a polite voice says to my left. Up close, Amos's eyes are just as compelling as his father's, but he's not so overbearing. He smiles, and without thinking, I smile back.

He bows slightly and then leads the way out of the large room and down a hallway. Seth is ahead of me, and I follow slowly behind him and Amos. We take several turns, until I'm confused by where we are, and then Amos stops in front of a door. "This is your room, Mei." He gestures with his hand.

I glance at Seth.

"Your companion will be just down the hallway," Amos says with an easy smile. "I'll return soon to see if everything is to your taste." He bows again, and one of the guards stations himself outside my door. I hesitate, but I really have no choice. Opening the door, I peer inside. It's beautiful. A large room with floor-to-ceiling windows along one side, gold and white curtains, a tiled floor, and a magnificent four-poster bed. Strange and beautiful artwork adorns the walls, and there's a luxurious woolen rug on the floor in the same blues and greens as a peacock's tail. I step onto the rug and curl my toes into the softness. I've never stayed anywhere like this before.

There's another room to one side, a bathroom. All of a sudden, I feel dirty. I shuffle into the room, checking for towels. There's a change of clothes, cotton pants and a shirt, even a bra and undies that are about my size. Part of me recoils at the idea that they know my size, but I'm so exhausted, I can't work myself into being outwardly upset over it. I pull off my dirty and ripped clothes, and step under the water. It's a double shower, so I turn on both heads and close my eyes as the water soaks my skin and rejuvenates me.

It's only when I start to sway that I get out of the shower. The big soft bed in the other room is calling to me. I need sleep, or I'm going to be useless. I dress in the clothes they've provided and wander back out into the main room, drying my hair with a towel. I spot a brush on a dresser near the bed and use it to take the worst of the knots out of my long tangled hair. I eye the bed for a moment, trying to work up the energy to avoid it. I give in and lay myself down. It's as soft as it looks, and I almost float on the thick duvet cover. As I'm drifting off to sleep, someone knocks on my door.

Sitting bolt upright, I remember where I am and why I'm here. I'm a prisoner, no matter that they've put me in the nicest prison anyone could ever have. I climb down off the bed and resolve to sleep on the floor to remind myself not to relax.

When I open the door, Amos is smiling at me, a tray of food in his hands. "May I come in?"

I step back and wave him in. "Sure. It's not like I have a choice, is it?"

A line appears between his eyes. "My father has high-handed methods, but he does it for the greater good. He wants you to feel welcome here."

It's hard not to remind him of all the people his father has killed trying to bring me here, but I hold it in. Amos seems friendly. Perhaps if I can befriend him, he'll help me. "Really?" is all I say, trying to put all my fear and frustration into that one word.

"Really," Amos says earnestly. "He just wants what is best for everyone."

"Maybe not everyone," I murmur under my breath. Turns out it's hard to be discrete.

Amos frowns, and I smile at him. "What food have you brought me? I'm starving. I haven't eaten since..." I trail off, remembering that Si was supposed to be cooking us dinner when they were attacked. I'm suddenly not hungry anymore.

"What is it?"

"Do you really want to know?" I ask in a tight voice.

"Of course. I wouldn't ask otherwise."

"My friend Si was cooking dinner when your father's mercenaries attacked and killed him, as well as my other mentor Jeff. So I haven't eaten in a while."

Amos's face darkens, and his brown eyes flash with an emotion I can't decipher. "I'm sorry about your friends. I didn't know they had been hurt."

"Then you're not in your father's confidence and you can't say for sure what he means to do with me," I snap. Inwardly I wince. I really did mean to be nice to him. He seems gentle compared to his father. It's almost like kicking a puppy.

"My father... has a very strong opinion on the way things should be, and he will do anything necessary to make sure it comes about," says Amos, his expression earnest. "We need people like him to make the tough decisions and ensure the peace. It's the only way."

This time I can't help it. I sneer at him. "That sounds like a rehearsed speech. How many times have you practiced that in the mirror?"

Amos carefully places the tray down on the dresser and turns back to me. Instead of anger on his face, I see sadness. "I'm sorry you feel that way. My father is a great man, you'll see. Once you're rested and have talked to him, you'll come to understand the way it must be."

He walks purposefully back to the door, and I notice for the first time that he moves with the quiet grace of someone who knows how to fight. It occurs to me that he's been raised in the middle of a war, just like me. I feel a weird kind of kinship with him, and when Amos opens the door and glances back at me one more time, I'm not feeling so angry anymore. Amos nods to me, then closes the door behind him with a quiet click.

But that small click is far more ominous than if he'd slammed it. I shiver, holding my arms around my body.

13

I wake up slowly, and at first, I can't remember where I am. I rub my hand over my eyes, wiping at the sleep in the corners. I look around the room and freeze.

I'm a prisoner of the Earthbound, stuck in some strange fortress, who knows where, at the mercy of a man who has been chasing me since I was a baby. For a moment, I'm motionless, holding the sheet against my body.

I feel like a deer in the headlights, and the thought flashes through my head that perhaps if I don't move from this spot, time will stand still and I'll be able to avoid the confrontation with Vincent that I know is coming. I'm frozen for a moment longer and then I sigh. When did hiding from things ever make them go away? I know that better than anyone.

I crawl out of bed and go stand next to the tray of food that Amos delivered. I didn't eat any last night, but now I'm so hungry I could gnaw my arm off. I pick up the fruit pieces and start to munch on them. The sandwiches have wilted a little, but I drink the orange juice and devour the crackers and cheese.

Just as I'm checking out the windows for latches—there are none—I hear a scratching at the door, and a guard opens it unceremoniously. "Vincent wants to see you," he says.

"I've just woken. I need to freshen up," I say, just to be perverse.

The guard nods. "You have five minutes to prepare yourself." He slams the door shut.

I consider delaying, but the guard looks the type to drag me down the hallway whether I'm wearing a towel or my clothes. The bathroom has a new toothbrush, deodorant, and soap. Everything a girl could want. Five minutes later, I'm ready to face the demon.

The guard opens the door, gesturing for me to follow. I look around the hallway, half expecting Seth to be there. "Is Seth coming too?"

The guard shakes his head. "No. He will remain in his room."

He leads me back to the same chambers as yesterday and I'm able to look around more coherently. The murals and paintings are still the most eye-catching aspect of the room. They're all depicting heroic acts of bravery by members of the Earthbound, who are wearing their ceremonial robes.

I can't help but give an incredulous snort.

The dragons are depicted as terrifying and diabolical beasts, but I feel sorry for them. The Dragon Wars were fought because of too many dragons and too little space. They were beautiful creatures, if deadly, and didn't deserve to be hunted to extinction by the Earthbound. They just needed a few lessons in birth control.

I don't deserve to be here either, hunted down by the Earthbound. I narrow my eyes and study a particularly gory painting of a dragon with its head severed from its neck. Given the purpose of the Earthbound, my being here doesn't make any sense. If Vincent really thinks I'm a dragon, he should have killed me when he had the chance. Which makes me wonder if he's just playing some kind of game with me.

What is he trying to achieve?

Staring into the painted eyes of a dragon in its last death throes, I can't imagine why anyone would think I'm linked to something so fierce and dangerous. If I'm a dragon, I'll eat my hat. I'm nothing like the wild creatures on the walls. Si was always trying to get me to be more ruthless, more fierce, when I fight. Maybe now I know why.

Thinking of Si and Jeff makes me clench my fists. I can't believe this all comes down to Vincent believing I'm a dragon. What a stupid mistake. It's almost too much to bear.

I look around, trying to distract myself. There's no one else in the room other than the guard, who has merged back into the wall behind me. On the side of the room, a door opens and two more guards enter the chamber, followed by Vincent. He waves me over to him and sits at a large chair. He gestures at one of the guards, who pulls another chair over to rest next to his. "Come, child, sit here with me. I will not hurt you."

Part of me wants to remain where I am, to see what he does. Will he send over one of his guards to manhandle me? But, instead I stride over and sit down purposefully, my eyes never leaving his. He stares back calmly, not seeming perturbed by my focused attention.

He doesn't say anything, and the silence makes me start to fidget. I'm the first to break the eye contact, and I see him smile. I realise it's a power play, and he feels he's won something. I don't like to tell him I could have kept going all day;

Jeff was the master of the stare-down. I just want to move things along.

"I promised to answer your questions," he says.

"You did."

He spreads his arms wide and leans back. "Ask away."

"Why have you really been hunting me all these years?"

"You still don't believe me? I do not lie."

"You've been misinformed." I glance up at the pictures of dead or dying dragons around the room. "I'm not one of those creatures. There's no way."

"There are many misconceptions about dragons now that they no longer inhabit our Earth. They take on two forms, human and dragon. Dragons are not simple creatures; they are intelligent, fierce, and complex. They have qualities of both their human side and their beast side."

"I'm none of those things. I'm pretty simple, actually." I have to convince him that I'm not who he thinks I am. Then perhaps he'll stop this relentless pursuit. Hope flares in my chest. Maybe I can escape this constant cat-and-mouse game?

"You're nothing like the dragons of old, you are correct. You weren't raised in one of their feral nests; you weren't taught the old ways from birth. But that doesn't mean you're not a dragon."

"Is my father a dragon too, then?" I ask.

"He is not. Dragons don't mate with other dragons. They cannot bear to be in each other's company for more than a few minutes. That is why the Dragon Wars were so devastating."

"So they mate with humans?"

"Your father hides it well, but he is not human either. Dragons must mate with supernaturals. A human could not do what was necessary to impregnate a dragon."

I scrunch up my face at his words. I can't believe he's talking about sex with me. He's a freaking stranger. Well, maybe not a stranger; he's been stalking me my whole life. That might make it worse.

"What makes you think I'm a dragon?"

Vincent settles back in his chair. "Your mother was the last of her kind; she had lain dormant for many centuries before emerging from her hiding place near the mouth of the Yangtze River in China. Your father was sent over to investigate sightings. But when he found her, he didn't do his duty and kill her." Vincent's lip curls. "Instead, they had a baby together."

"Just like that?" It's a nice story, but I can't afford to believe anything this man tells me.

Vincent waves his hand. "Oh, months passed. We waited patiently, thinking he was simply being thorough. But then we realised he wasn't planning to come back." Vincent paused, staring off into the distance.

"Then what happened?" I say impatiently.

"She had just had a baby when we attacked. Your father wasn't at the house. She was holed up in her fortress in China for five days before erupting out of it and fighting the Earthbound to the death. The baby was never found."

"What makes you think I'm that baby?"

"Your father married her in secret. When he appeared back in the US with a baby, we knew immediately who you were."

"And you tried to kill me."

He pauses before answering, glancing away and back again. "I promised to tell you the truth. So yes, we did try to kill you. We tried for a few years when you were a child. But then we realized what you could do."

"And what's that?"

"You can help sustain the spell web. You're more powerful than any other supernatural alive, and your magic alone could keep the spell web operating smoothly for *years*."

"If I'm so powerful, how come you captured me?" I ask snarkily. I still have the bruises to show from it.

"You did manage to knock out all my men. You're a young woman alone, without her usual protectors, and you haven't been introduced to your dragon side yet. I'm an older, more experienced opponent."

I roll my eyes at him.

He shrugs, as if he is not responsible for his supposed advantage.

"And how do I charge up the spell web?"

"I believe you already have a strong connection to it. I've been watching the spikes in the spell web around you since you arrived. You've used it unconsciously the whole time, testing things out, sensing what is happening around you. You would just need to tap into that a little more." He flicks his fingers and I realize he's lying to me.

Those hours of playing poker with Jeff are finally paying off. Vincent twitches. I've seen it twice in this conversation. Once when he told me he wouldn't hurt me, and now talking about how I would power the spell web. What makes me think he's lying? I don't know, but I don't trust him.

I think of Jeff and his arguments against the spell web. "Why do we need the spell web anymore? There are no more dragons."

"We have you."

"Answer the question."

He sighs. "The last three hundred years have been the most peaceful on record for the supernatural community.

The ability of the spell web to hide supernaturals from the humans has proved to be a positive outcome. We don't have to contend with their fear and their conspiracy theories on a daily basis. We're free to live our lives."

"Is it fair to the humans?"

"Do you honestly think they want to know that werewolves, dragons, and other monsters really exist? No, of course not. They're much happier now than they would be if they knew."

"And you're going to decide that for them?"

"Absolutely. Along with the SIG, who are completely comfortable with the idea."

"So why do you need me? Isn't the spell web self-sustaining?"

Again he pauses. His fingers twitch. "The magic of the spell web is weakening. The number of supernaturals is declining; there are gaps appearing in the spell web."

I think of Seth and wonder if he's a gap that shouldn't be there. His patchy coverage is unusual, but I don't think it's a weakening in the spell web. It feels more like a natural occurrence, like someone who doesn't quite fit into the web as it's been designed.

I send out a whisper along the spell web, looking for evidence of what Vincent is saying to me. Straight away, I find breakages around us, weakened areas I've never felt before. I've never felt it anywhere else, and I wonder what has been happening at the Earthbound headquarters to cause such weakness in the web. One thing is for sure, Vincent is not telling me the whole truth.

"I can sense you along the spell web. You play with it like it's a toy." His voice has an edge to it, and I'm confused, until I realize he's jealous.

He's the Earthbound leader; he's supposed to be the one controlling the spell web.

"I still don't get why you're so sure I'm a dragon."

"I can see you're not going to believe it unless I prove it to you. Come with me."

"Where are we going?"

"To try to kill you."

14

My heart pounds in my chest as I struggle against the two guards. The massive see-through container of water looms below me. There are bricks strapped to my sides, making it difficult to move. Plus, they're supers, and my extra strength isn't more than the two of them combined.

They're going to drown me. Vincent is officially fucking crazy.

Who has this kind of thing lying around anyway? A big see-thru box of water. There's no air inside it, just water, and they're going to close the lid over me. I love water, I always have, but that doesn't change the fact that I'll drown in minutes. This has been his plan all along, and I wasted time talking to him, trying to understand what he was doing. I could have escaped while I was in that damn room.

It makes me want to scream.

When they suddenly let go, I plunge straight down into the water. I land at the bottom of the pool with a thud and immediately look around. Vincent and the guards are watching me like I'm some kind of science experiment. I desperately attempt to untie the bricks from around my waist, but my movements are thick and clunky, and I can't get them free. Water is my element, but it feels like my enemy today. I don't know what Vincent expects me to do.

Maybe it's like those witch trials from centuries ago: drop the woman in water, if she lives, she's a witch—or a dragon—if she drowns, she isn't a witch—or a dragon.

Whichever way it goes, I think I'm going to lose.

A low sound comes out my mouth, sending bubbles up to the surface. Damned if I'm going to lose. To paraphrase Seth, it's time to turn the situation around. I search the small space for a weakness, somewhere I can force myself free. I have water magic, after all. I should be able to use it.

I kick up to the top of the pool, the weight of the bricks making it difficult, and push with my shoulder against the door where they let me in. It doesn't budge. I swim to the corners and shove against the join where the panes of glass meet. I gather my magic around me, thrusting the water at the glass as well. There is some kind of spell holding it all together, and my magic can't break through.

I'm running out of air. I hit the glass repeatedly with the palm of my hands in front of Vincent, trying to let him know that I give in. That he wins and I'm wrong. If he wants me to be a dragon, then I will damn well be a dragon.

As long as he doesn't let me drown in this stupid box of water.

But Vincent simply watches me, his face impassive. He's waiting for me to do something amazing, and I can't. I'm not who he thinks I am. I've been waiting my whole life to find out why they're hunting me, and now that I know, I realize it's all been a mistake. I'm not special.

I'm not a dragon.

I kick at the glass, my anger building, covering over the

despair. Who the hell does he think he is? He's going to kill me to prove a point.

My hands move to the ropes at my waist, and I pull at them again. This time, my anger clears my mind and makes me focus. I manage to pull one of the bricks away from the rope.

It's an immediate relief.

Turning, I slam the brick into the glass wall of the pool. I use all my strength, pushing my whole body into the movement. The glass doesn't crack, but it makes a mark. I slam the brick a second time, and a tiny chink appears. A third and fourth attack on the glass don't result in much, but the fifth time, the glass cracks.

Everything is slowed down underwater, and the liquid pushes against me like it doesn't want me to escape. I soothe it, pushing out messages into the water surrounding me. I tell it that I need to get out to survive. That I'll die if I don't. And just like that, something changes. The water is helping me, sending waves toward the crack, pushing itself against the newly formed hole and trying to get out.

I'm desperate for air and slam the brick down against the glass with everything I have. I see stars, and my vision starts to narrow, but the crack is no bigger.

I have nothing left. I lean against the glass wall and wonder what it's like to drown.

And then, without warning, a large air bubble appears next to me. It moves over my face until it covers my nose, giving me air. I gulp it in, unable to be moderate. The water is helping me and I'm not going to reject it.

The air reminds me what I'm doing here. I slam my brick against the glass wall one more time. The crack widens and water gushes out. I swim to the top, inhaling air from the gap forming at the top. I stay there while the water continues to gush out through the crack in the side.

I can see Vincent frowning up at me, and I know I haven't done what he expected me to. Perhaps he wanted me to drown. He gestures at the guards. They run around the side of the pool, up the stairs, and open the trap door at the top. I swim over, and they pull me out.

"Happy now?" I ask angrily. "What were you expecting?"

"For you to breathe the water. Dragons can breathe both air and water. They have the internal systems to get the oxygen they need from both substances."

"Are you convinced I'm not a dragon now?"

"Strangely no." He stares at me with his intense blue eyes. "We'll do another test."

The guards grab my arms as the words sink in. He's starting to doubt himself. "If I don't pass this next test, will you let me go?"

"Oh no. If you don't pass this next test, you'll be dead." He glances at me, a frown marring his features. "I'm sure you'll be fine."

I'm sure I won't.

15

They've locked me in a stone room.

No windows, nothing that isn't stone. I know it's underground, because they led me down from the pool, but that's all I'm sure of. It's dry, not at all damp, but I can see small round openings on the roof, like water sprinklers.

I have a terrible feeling they aren't sprinklers.

My brain is whirring, and I'm almost dizzy with the number of possibilities for how he's going to kill me. I'm so busy being scared that I don't notice the heat rising at first.

It's only when I wipe sweat away from my forehead that I notice what's happening. I glance up and see the wavy air as heat blasts through the tubes in the ceiling.

Heat is fine, I can handle hot. Si always says I'm almost as much a lizard as he is, and he's a chameleon, so that's saying something. But there's a limit. I was never impervious.

Not like a dragon would be.

When fire erupts through the ceiling vents, I scream. I can't help myself. Vincent wasn't lying when he said I'd emerge a dragon or dead. My only option is death at this point.

But there's something in me that won't stay down, and I start hunting around the walls of the room, avoiding the fire blasts, trying to find an exit door, a way out. On my fifth circumference of the room, I slam my hand into the stone and admit defeat. This place is sealed tight. There's no water to help me escape this time.

Again the anger surges up in me. Who does he think he is? He doesn't have the right to decide life or death, particularly mine.

I send out a tendril over the spell web, and am surprised to find it hearty and strong beside me in here. I had half-expected Vincent to have some secret way of blocking me from it. I think of the men he sent to capture me, and the extra magic they gathered from the web around them. Can I do that as well?

It can't hurt to try. I'm going to die if I don't do something.

I'm not entirely certain how to pull magic from the web, so I start by connecting myself to the area around me, sending feelers out, drawing it in closer. As I draw it in, I sense the energy around me, and I pull at it. It comes easily, and I'm shocked. I hadn't really expected this to work.

I drag it closer and closer, until I feel a buildup of the spell web around me like a wall. I wrap it over me, hardening it until it's like a physical presence, and not simply the glowing grid I normally see.

I'm cooler now; the heat can't get through my protective barrier. I take a few deep breaths, and then realize the other problem with this scenario. I might be cooler, but the fire will burn up all the oxygen, and soon I won't have any air to breathe. I need to get out of here, fast.

But I've already checked, haven't I? There's no way out.

I slump down onto the uneven stones beneath me. Tears form in my throat. At least the people I love will stop being killed on my behalf. No one else will die because of me.

A pebble wriggles under my butt, and I lean over to sweep it away. Another loose pebble shifts under me, and I sweep it away too. Then I move over and look properly at the small patch of pebbles and stones in this corner. They're all loose and crumbling.

My breath hitches.

I start clawing at the stones on the floor. Not much happens. I keep grabbing at the stone until I notice the tips of my fingers are bloodied and scratched. I look at them like they belong to someone else, and maybe they do. It doesn't hurt, nothing hurts, because I'm about to be burned alive down here. The protection barrier won't last forever; I can already feel myself heating up again. A sob escapes and I hold the back of my hand against my mouth. My magic is already weakening.

And then I hear Seth's voice in my head again. *We need to turn this situation around.*

What else can I try? The spell web is protecting me from behind, but...

Quickly, I gather magic from the grid and push it at the stone surface. The stone peels away like orange skin. I can't help but gape down at the stone, wondering how that's even possible. There's a flare of heat behind me as the spell web barrier weakens. I need to hurry; it's going to break. I'm taking too much magic from the barrier keeping the heat at bay.

The surface below is metal. Maybe there's no way out. Maybe it's all just metal under here. But I keep moving the stone floor until I find a handle. There's just a tiny door in one corner. I pull on it, but it doesn't budge.

But I'm not taking no for an answer, and I pull again, using all my might. It moves slightly. Not locked, just pulled tight. Hope flares in my chest and I pull with both hands on the latch, grunting with the effort.

When it eventually comes free, I fly back into the wall, smacking my shoulder against the stone. I don't even care, because there's a way out, and I'm taking it. I climb down a ladder into the darkness below and take a deep breath of air. It's stale and damp, with undertones of sewage, but at least it's oxygen.

I close the trap door and sneak along the narrow stone tunnel. There's mould and moss on the walls, and it's clear that no one has been down here in a long time. I feel a whisper of cool air brushing against my cheek, hinting at a way out. If Seth wasn't hidden somewhere here, locked up in his chamber, I might just follow this tunnel out of here.

But I can't. I have to find Seth and get him out of here too.

I have no idea of my bearings, so I just pick a direction and walk. I'm hoping this is some kind of underground tunnel system that's going to let me roam underneath the Earthbound facility.

It won't be long until they figure out that I'm not burned to a crisp in there. Then they'll be searching for me. The thought makes me walk a little faster, my heart pounding as I wonder what Vincent would do to me next. My feet move faster and faster, until I'm running down the stone tunnel, heedless to who might hear me or which direction I'm going.

Running is the only way I can free myself from the terrible visions of being burned alive, or being caught again so they can try some new method of killing me. My breath is ragged and uneven, and my body aches all over, but I keep going, unable to stop. I come to a T-junction and turn left, with no real knowledge of where I should be going.

Eventually my need to get away from the burning room calms down. I slow to a walk, lungs heaving in and out, my hands on my hips as I try to regain my equilibrium.

I have to get out of the tunnels and back up into the main building. I need to find Seth and get out of here.

Up ahead I see a light. As I get closer, it becomes a lantern that has been placed beside a door.

I hesitate with one hand over the handle. It could be another trap, a way for Vincent to mess with me in his efforts to prove he's right.

But that's not rational. How could Vincent possibly know I would escape? He was expecting me to use my non-existent dragon powers to protect myself. I don't even know enough about dragons to know what powers that might include. Maybe scales like Si's that appeared when he needed them most.

Turning the handle, I peer past the door into a darkened hallway. It seems drier, less smelly, than the tunnel I'm in. I'm pretty sure I'm at the basement level, so I need to get higher. I cautiously step out, looking up and down. There's a light down to the left, so for lack of a better plan, I head that way.

As I'm getting closer, I sense another supernatural through the web, and push myself against the wall. I'm shaking so hard my body is vibrating against the stone surface behind me—I need someone to give me a slap and tell me to harden the hell up.

A guard enters the corridor from another adjoining one. He doesn't look my way, just turns in the opposite direction and strides down the hall. He turns at another junction, and then he's out of sight. I sigh with relief.

I peer around the edge of the corridor that he came from, but there's no one else there. Hopefully he's doing some kind of regular circuit and he's not due back for a while. I run down the corridor, trying to be as quiet as I can, until I find a set of stairs. By this time, I'm shaking so badly I'm not sure I'm going to be able to make it up. But I have no choice.

I've gone up three flights before I find a level that looks familiar. The same floor-to-ceiling murals of the dead and dying dragons that were in Vincent's big hall are on the walls. I open the door from the stairwell onto this level and immediately close it again as three guards march around the corner.

I crouch down in the stairwell, away from the small glass viewing hole on the door, but the guards don't even peer through. They're going somewhere, not doing rounds.

Opening the door again, I race along the hallway, trying to run as quietly as I can. I'm not entirely sure where I am, until I see the large suit of armor outside the double doors to Vincent's chambers. All the air leaves my lungs at once, and I almost trip over my own legs. Standing up suddenly seems too hard. I can't see Vincent again.

I can't.

I take a couple of deep breaths. I can hear Jeff telling me off. *Being scared won't help. You have to fight to get out of there.*

Vincent doesn't even know I'm here.

I run along the hallway, trying desperately to recall the route back to the room they kept me in. After a couple of false starts, I end up in front of the door. I'm tempted to go back inside and clean myself off, but that feels too much like re-entering my prison, and I can't bring myself to do it.

I half run along the hallway, trying all the doors along the way. Eventually I come to a room that's not locked and open the door. Seth isn't inside. I don't know why I thought he'd be inside an unlocked room. Instead, there's a large desk, and Amos is sitting in front of a laptop, wire-rimmed glasses dipping low on his nose.

"Mei. It's lovely to see you," he says, smiling at me. "What are you doing here?"

I take a breath and decide to take a terrible risk. "Your father just tried to kill me. Twice. He's convinced that I'm a dragon, and I'm really not. Amos, you need to help me get out of here." I walk up to him, holding out my burned hands. I lift my shirt and show him the raw skin where the ropes holding the bricks rubbed my body.

Amos looks at my hands and side. "He was so sure..." he says, almost to himself. He looks up into my eyes. "He promised me that he'd give you a few days to get used to the idea, to come to terms with it before he threw you in the deep end."

"You knew what he was planning?" My blood begins to boil, and I feel my magic surge to the surface, burning to get out.

"Only if you proved difficult to convince. He was sure it was a stage you wouldn't get to."

"He wanted to test me?" My hands are clammy. Amos knew what his father was planning. He'd condoned it. I walk slowly backward to the door.

"Yes. He was so sure you'd be able to get out of those ropes and escape with no harm done." He glances at my burned and bloodied body. "But you didn't, did you?"

I shake my head. "I got out of his torture chambers, but no thanks to your father. Or my non-existent dragon powers." It's clear I'm not going to get any help from Amos. I'd hoped he didn't know. I turn to leave.

"Wait, Mei. Where are you going?"

"To find Seth." *And get out of here.*

"I can show you where he is." He pauses. "And then show you the way out."

16

I'm following Amos at a distance. If it turns out he's lying, I think I can outrun him from this far back. I don't understand why he's helping me—more likely he's leading me back to his father. Why would he do anything else? But he leads me down a narrow corridor, through a doorway, and down a set of stone stairs to a row of rooms very different to where I was staying.

"Are these prison cells?" I ask.

A flush appears across Amos's cheeks. "My father felt the SIG agent needed a closer watch on him."

"I thought *I* was the dangerous dragon?"

"He's also annoyed at the SIG for breaking their agreement with the Earthbound. He's known for a long time, and he can use the SIG agent to prove it was happening. He wants compensation."

"Blackmail."

"Concessions for bad behavior."

"I'm pretty sure killing people counts as bad behavior." In my head I see Jeff lying in a pool of blood. Si being shot.

Amos stops suddenly, and I almost crash into him. "The

deaths of your mentors are regrettable. I don't condone that." He looks down at me with his serious expression, his soft brown eyes showing his concern.

"Your father does." I hold my ground, unwilling to give an inch, despite his puppy-dog eyes.

Amos nods. "Yes. My father's methods are increasingly brutal. He's concerned that your twentieth birthday is fast approaching."

"Ah, yes, the biggest birthday on the supernatural calendar. What does your father think will happen to me?"

"He believes you will come into your full powers as a dragon."

"And is he ever going to let me be?" I ask. "Or is he going to force me to help with this crazy scheme of his?"

"He hopes you will join him in his quest to ensure the spell web remains in place. If you don't, he has calculated that it will be destroyed in less than five years."

I pause. The thought of the spell web being destroyed leaves me breathless. The spell web is what allows me to function. It's like a fifth limb, and I can't imagine being without it. Little flutters of panic jump to life in the depths of my stomach. It's my last line of defense, the ace up my sleeve. Maybe I should consider Vincent's offer?

I let out a frustrated breath. I'm not a dragon, and never will be, so there's no point.

Even if I was, I remind myself of the methods Vincent has used. "He killed the two men in my life who were like my fathers."

Amos hesitates. "I'm sure it was a mistake. But I'll help you. Don't worry."

It's on the tip of my tongue to say it wasn't a mistake, that his father admitted as much to me in our little talk. But getting into an argument with Amos won't get me out of here, so I keep quiet.

Amos leads me to a locked door and pulls out a key. Inside, Seth is sitting on a narrow bed, reading a book. He looks up in surprise.

"Seth, are you okay?" I push past Amos to get to him.

He stands up and wraps me into a tight hug. "They wouldn't tell me what was happening or where you were. Are you okay?" he says, staring down at my face.

I nod, crossing my fingers childishly. "We're getting out of here. Amos is helping us."

He glances over at Amos, his eyes narrowing. "Then let's go."

We head off at a run, back up the stairs, and down another side corridor. I'm glad Amos knows where we're going. About five minutes later, a loud siren starts up. I cover my ears.

"They've realized you're out," puffs Amos. "We need to hurry."

He leads us to a side door near the kitchens and opens it with a flourish. We're in a courtyard with a small VW van to one side. Amos unlocks it and pulls open the side door. "You'll need to lie down in the back. Under the blanket," Amos says. He climbs into the driver's seat and has the van started before we're even inside. "Hurry," he urges.

The van has a soft, stuffed-pillow mattress covering most of it, so it's not as uncomfortable as it could have been. Lying down on the pillows, I pull the huge, dark blue blanket over me. Its musty scent fills my nose, and I try not to sneeze.

Seth hesitates, still standing in the doorway. His hazel eyes flash with gold in the afternoon sun. Then he slowly climbs into the van and lies down next to me, pulling the blanket over his head. It immediately feels too hot under the scratchy material, his large warm body touching mine.

Amos is already driving the van down the road toward the massive guard station.

I try to get comfortable, but I'm just fidgeting. Seth grabs me and puts both arms around me, holding me against his chest. I lean my head on his shoulder.

"Hold still," he whispers in my ear. His warm breath tickles my skin and I shiver. I hold my breath, trying to follow his order.

"Thanks for getting me out," he says. "You could have left me there."

I shake my head. "I wouldn't do that."

"Not everyone thinks like that. So, thanks."

Then we're stopped at the guard station, and we both go completely still.

I don't know if we can trust Amos. This is a huge risk. Why the hell would he go against his father for some stranger? The more I think about it, the less it makes sense. I'm suddenly convinced that it's all a ploy to make me more vulnerable or willing to cooperate.

I start breathing heavily. The blanket is scratching at my skin, making me want to itch. It's too hot under here, and all I want to do is push off the blanket and suck in some fresh air.

Seth tightens his hold on me, like he knows what I'm thinking.

Amos is talking to the guard, and they both laugh. This is it. The point where they tell us it's all been a joke, and we're not really free. Pressing my face against Seth's neck, I hold myself rigid, frightened that if I even move an inch, I'll end up giving us away.

Then the van starts up and we're through.

I let out a breath, and Seth squeezes my hand. My whole body is shaking, I'm so relieved to be free of that place. I can't quite bring myself to be the one to break away from Seth. His comforting warmth is the only thing that saved me from bursting out of the van and making a stupid, desperate run for it back there.

Amos drives for another few miles before he slows down next to a service station. I reluctantly pull away from Seth. Amos parks to one side of the station and gets into the back of the van, closing the door behind him. By this time, Seth and I are sitting opposite each other on the cushions and Amos makes himself comfortable next to me.

"Why did you do it?" I ask him. I'm still trembling and I need something to distract me.

Amos shrugs. "I couldn't let my father hurt you. It's not right."

"He's wrong about me, you know." Even now, I need to convince him. To make sure he understands that he's done the right thing.

Amos glances at my face and then away again. He nods. "That's what I'm counting on."

"So what now?" I ask.

He shakes his head, his black curls bouncing over his face. "I don't know. My father will be angry."

"That's an understatement," says Seth softly, his eyes flashing, even in the dim light of the van.

Amos goes pale, like he's only just realizing what he's done, and I glare at Seth. He's not making this any easier.

Impulsively I put one hand on Amos's arm. "Thank you. You saved my life today."

He looks at me; there's warmth in his eyes that wasn't there before. He smiles and puts his hand over mine. "As soon as I saw you, I knew you could never hurt anyone."

I'm a little taken aback by his statement. He barely knows me, but he's somehow romanticized me into someone I'm not. His skin feels clammy, and he's holding my hand tightly in place. I wish I hadn't touched him. "I promise I'm really not who your father thinks I am. Setting me on fire isn't going to change that." I pull my hand away gently. Amos's smile falters and he looks hurt, but I can't help that.

Seth looks at me, his eyes narrowed. "What the hell happened back there?"

"Vincent tried to prove I'm a dragon." I try to look calm, like it was nothing. But the memory of the burning hot room makes me flush with heat.

"How?" he asks suspiciously. He looks at my singed clothing more closely.

I hold my hands in my lap to stop the tremors. "I got out, that's all that matters. But let's just say I don't plan on going back."

17

We're heading east.

I don't know if Amos has figured out why, but both Seth and I are aiming for New York. It's the head office of the SIG, and hopefully my father is there. I don't expect the rank and file at the SIG to know or help me, but my father will get me out of this mess.

I hope.

I glance at Amos next to me in the driver's seat. He's concentrating on the road, and ignores me. He's a very conscientious driver. I get the impression he hasn't driven much before. Seth is in the back, trying to sleep.

Now I know what Vincent has been looking for all these years, I feel stupid. Angry, too. But mostly stupid, because I can't do the things he wants me to. He's waiting for me to set everything on fire, and I can't. To swim without needing to breathe. It's like being asked to recite the alphabet backwards in school and realizing you don't even know it forwards.

"So this is your van, huh?" I say to Amos. "It's nice." Ever since I pulled away from his hand, he's been distant. I don't want to hurt his feelings, and we owe him a huge debt.

Amos nods. "I bought it a few years ago. When I still thought I might be allowed to go to college one day." His voice has a tinge of bitterness.

"Your dad doesn't approve?"

"He believes in saving the world. That's about it. Doesn't leave much time for the normal stuff."

I nod. "I know what that's like. We had to move around all the time, to keep off the trail of... your father." I glance at Amos. "I never had much time to be normal either."

In the back, Seth snorts. "Normal is overrated. Ask anyone."

Amos and I lock eyes. Seth doesn't understand the isolation of being a child caught up in something like this. On this point, Amos and I understand each other completely.

"Do you think your father will forgive you?" I ask tentatively. From what I've seen, I don't think so.

Amos clenches his hands on the steering wheel. "If it turns out you really are a dragon, then no. But if you're not" —he glances at me—"then I might be okay."

I hold one hand over my heart. "I promise I'm not a dragon." I'm certain of it now we've left the Earthbound stronghold. I think back to the ferocious dragon paintings that lined the halls. "Not even remotely."

Amos gives me a relieved smile. "I'm going to get you as far away from the Earthbound as I can, give him a chance to cool off. Dad can be overbearing sometimes, but he does it for all the best reasons."

I nod, but I don't agree with him. His father is caught up in his version of the way things should be. I don't want the spell web to come down, but I don't think it has to be me who keeps it alive. Or that he should be allowed to force me to do it.

"Perhaps I could talk to my father? Make him see reason. You could come back to the Earthbound sanctuary and help us," Amos suggests. He doesn't take his eyes off the road, but I can see the tension in his face and I think he's holding his breath.

I shake my head abruptly, too horrified to be tactful. "Your father has been trying to kill or capture me my entire life. His people have murdered almost all the people in my life who meant anything to me. He just tried to kill me—twice. I can't just make friends and pretend none of that happened," I say fiercely.

Amos glances at me, his eyes wide. He immediately turns back to the road. His face is flushed. "I... I'm sorry. I didn't think of it like that."

"I'm not trying to upset you, Amos," I say, and I really mean it. I don't want to hurt his feelings. We'd never have escaped without him, and he seems like a decent person.

But he has to understand his father is the bad guy here.

The worst of it is that Vincent has been focused on the wrong person all these years. I'm not a dragon. Which means there might be someone else out there who is. Was the story Vincent told me about the Chinese dragon's baby even true? Goose bumps rise over my skin. What if they found me somewhere, a supernatural child with no parents, and put me in as a decoy to distract Vincent?

Am I a decoy-dragon?

Maybe all these years, the reason my father hasn't been that interested in me is because I'm not really his daughter. Perhaps I was never even expected to survive this long? Was I supposed to die young and convince Vincent he'd won?

I could be like those kids who are born to be stem cell

donors to their sick brothers or sisters. My sole purpose in life is to be a decoy to the real dragon child.

For some reason, this hits me hard. I don't want to be disposable, the decoy for the real child. My stomach feels as if it's been punched, and tears fill my eyes. I grab a pair of sunglasses from the dashboard, and hide behind the reflective lenses. I clench my hands into shaking fists and try to convince myself I'm wrong.

But it really feels like it might be the truth.

Why else does Vincent think I'm a dragon, when I'm so clearly not? The answer seems obvious now. He's been conned. They've played the old switcheroo on him, and he doesn't even know it. I wonder where she is, the real dragon girl, and what she's doing. Does she have protectors like Si and Jeff keeping her alive? Does she have to move around all the time like me? Or is she living somewhere nice, secure in the knowledge that I'm taking the knocks so she won't have to?

I dig my nails into my palms and look out the window. It's just fields and fields of crops, as far as the eye can see. It's soothing, and I concentrate on identifying the different plants, just to keep my mind off this new insight.

"Was it truly that bad? Growing up?" Amos asks quietly.

I'm no longer in the mood to spare him. "We travelled a lot. Got attacked a lot. People died around me all the time. But after Jeff arrived when I was about seven, he found a way to predict the attacks. He learned the pattern of them, he used to say." I shake my head. "Whatever it was, it worked. We were still attacked all the time, but no one died. At least not after my protector Lee died when I was twelve." I glance at Amos, not willing to let him off the hook. "Until two days ago, when they killed two men who were like fathers to me. Just so they could get to me."

Amos runs one shaking hand through his mess of curly hair. "I'm sorry. He kept me away from the darker side of what he was doing."

"What was it like growing up with the Earthbound?" I ask, suddenly curious.

"My father is... intense. He's focused on one thing: protecting the spell web." Amos glances at me. "He's very good at it."

"Jeff said Vincent thought I was going to destroy the spell web when I turn twenty. But that's not true, is it?"

Amos shakes his head. "No. The spell web is dying and my father is convinced you're the only one who can save it. He thinks a dragon is the only supernatural strong enough."

"Why's the spell web dying?"

"Fewer supernaturals being born, and those being born aren't as strong."

"Why?"

"We don't know," he says, shaking his head.

I consider what he's saying for a few moments. "I'm already connected to the spell web. I'm obviously not enough to save it."

"You're not a dragon," Amos reminds me quietly.

I nod. He's right. "But if this dragon really had a baby all those years ago, wouldn't the real dragon baby be connected to the web as well?"

"They wouldn't be a full dragon yet and probably won't know how to wield their powers properly with no other dragons to teach them. My father has been studying the old confiscated dragon texts and believes he knows how to do it."

"So Vincent wants to use my supposed powerful dragon magic to keep the spell web going and maintain his own powerful position?"

"No, no, it's not like that," says Amos, his voice almost squeaking in protest. The van swerves a little on the road as he turns to me. "He's protecting the people from the darkness that surrounds them." The words slip easily out of his mouth and I know it's a phrase he's heard before.

"Protecting the humans, you mean? And supernaturals, we're the darkness?"

"Stop deliberately misunderstanding what I'm saying. You have to admit, not all supers are good for the human race."

"Not all *humans* are good for the human race," I retort.

"The Earthbound want to protect people, human *and* supernatural. Our world has been a better place since the creation of the spell web. Humans can live without constant fear, and supers can go about their daily lives without being lynched." His voice takes on a different tone, and for a moment he sounds just like his father. "It's what's best for everyone, even if they don't know it."

I stare hard at him, my heart beating fast. For a moment it was like Vincent was in the van with me. Have I made a terrible mistake, trusting Amos like this?

But Amos's expression is nothing like his father's—he's sincere and earnest as he tries to convince me. I take a deep breath and shake it off. Amos is not like his father. "I don't want the spell web to come down," I say. "That's not what I'm arguing for. I just don't think your father should be allowed to go around doing whatever he likes. What did I ever do to him?"

"It's not personal. He thought you could save the world. It's not his fault he was wrong."

"It's not my fault either. Or Jeff's. Or Si's." I look out the window, trying not to see all the blood. "What did any of us ever do, other than get in your father's way?"

"I'm truly sorry for what's happened to you, Mei. I really am." His voice breaks.

I turn to face him and see tears hovering in his soft brown eyes. Amos is truly upset. More importantly he's not to blame for his father's actions. I manage a small half-smile in his direction. "I appreciate it, Amos."

He turns back to the road, wiping at his eyes with the back of one hand. Neither of us can think of anything more to say and an awkward silence stretches across the front seat. I turn back to the window and watch the scenery pass by, thinking about what he's said.

The spell web is dying.

If I *were* the last dragon, I'd be happy to save it—although not in league with Vincent. I'd do it on my own. As I'm not the last dragon, perhaps there's a way to find the real dragon and convince her to save it instead?

18

A couple of hours later, Amos pulls into a service station, and I sit up, stretching my hands over my head. I'd been half asleep, lying with my head on my sweatshirt.

He glances at me, his expression nervy. "We need gas," he says, and climbs out of the van.

I sigh. He's clearly been driving and thinking about his father and what he's done by helping me escape; not to mention how much trouble he's going to be in when he gets back.

If he can ever go back.

I can't help him with that. It was his decision to help me and to come with us. I consider telling him he should stay away from his father for good. Maybe that way he can avoid the crazy-bug that seems to have infected Vincent.

I *could* say to Amos that he should move out from under his father's shadow and make a life for himself. But I don't. It's none of my business, and I don't think Amos would listen to me anyway. I just can't help feeling it's going to end badly for him. Goose bumps rise up over my arms.

I smooth down the fine hairs on one arm. Turning, I check on Seth in the back. He's curled up under the blanket, still asleep. How on earth he can sleep so soundly?

I climb out of the van as quietly as I can and head to the small shop. I still have a credit card, sewn into the lining of my trousers, and I don't think it's one the Earthbound can trace. If the SIG can find me using it, great. I still want to talk to them.

I grab a few snacks and drinks randomly off the shelves and head to the counter. Amos is ahead of me in the line talking to someone on his mobile phone. He seems calm, so I figure it's not his father.

I'm daydreaming about taking a hot shower, or even finding a river to swim in, when I glance outside toward the van. There's someone sneaking around the side, holding what looks like a Taser gun. I stare for a moment, not really believing my eyes.

Seth.

I run straight out the door, dropping all the food in my arms onto the floor. Just as the man is about to open the van, I launch myself at him, loading a punch to the head and firing it off.

He slams into the van and then slides down the side. A noise behind me warns me about a second attacker, and I spin, launching a backward roundhouse kick at chest height. It hits the second attacker in the stomach, and he steps back, but doesn't go down like the first man. I look up. He's tall, practically a sodding giant. He's brown-skinned with a shaggy mop of hair surrounding deep brown eyes and a craggy face. He's also covered in the glow of the spell web.

He grins down at me. "Hello, little girl. Do you want a

fight?" His voice is gravelly, like how a mountain might talk if it could.

He's a damn mountain supernatural. Hard as rock and twice as strong. Like most supernaturals, they can hide in plain sight in front of the humans, but they're on the borderline. He's tall and rugged and will probably beat me to a pulp.

I've never had to fight one, but Si has talked me through most types of supernatural creatures—the main ones he knew about anyway—and how to hurt them in a pinch. But a mountain super? *Damn things are impossible to kill, impossible to fight.*

I kick him again, just to be sure. I'm pretty sure it hurts me more than him. He grins, grabs my leg, and flips me to the ground. There's nothing I can do to stop him, he's so fast and strong. He pins me to the concrete. I struggle, striking at him with my legs and hands, but he doesn't move.

Mountain supers have the best of everything. They're strong, fast, smart, and don't feel pain. The only thing the rest of the world has going for us is that they hate other people—humans and supernaturals alike—and only want to hide away deep in the mountains.

Somehow, Vincent has convinced this mountain super to leave his preferred habitat to hunt me. "I'm not who he thinks I am, you know," I say desperately. I kick out with my leg, trying to make him lose his balance.

He doesn't even blink. "What makes you think I work for him?"

"Don't you?" I'm panting hard, trying to get my breath back. He doesn't even seem to be breaking a sweat.

He shrugs. "Sure I do."

"I'm not who he thinks," I say again.

He grins. "And what's that, little missy?" He pulls me to

my feet and holds me dangling in the air by my shirt. I grab a hold of his enormous hand, struggling to avoid being strangled, however accidentally.

"He thinks I'm a dragon. But I'm not." I swing and try to kick him in the side. He moves back easily.

The mountain super laughs, a deep rumbling sound that I might have liked if he hadn't been about to take me back to Vincent. "You're everything he says you are."

I roll my eyes. "He tested me. I failed both tests," I say. I swing again, this time wrapping my legs around his middle. I squeeze for all I'm worth. He doesn't seem to notice.

He starts walking toward a car with darkened windows, still holding my shirt with one hand. "I can feel the dragon in you, restin', waitin'," he says.

"You're crazy. You've taken one too many hits to the head." What's strange about this whole situation is that I'm actually starting to like him. He's got a nice face, a friendly expression with laugh lines that mean he could be called merry and jovial. There's something warm and approachable about him that I find appealing. It surprises me. I always thought a mountain supernatural would be grumpy and nasty.

It's not like I've known him for long either. Two minutes, and I get a crush.

"It's always been that way, with the mountains and the dragons. We're connected," he says in his rumbly voice.

"What?"

He's still holding my shirt, and I'm still clinging onto his arm and around his generous middle. "I can read your thoughts, if you let me. You don't know how to block me out, do you?"

My eyes widen, and I almost drop my hold. He casually grabs me with his other hand and swings me over his shoulder. I try to resist, but it's like trying to resist an avalanche, or a landslide. Or a brick wall.

"Why are you working for him? For Vincent?"

The big man hesitates, pausing in his steps. "It's complicated." His face darkens, and I feel a growl through his chest.

The rumbling noise sets off a connection in my head, and I push out along the spell web, trying to see if there is a way to beat him through it.

He's under the spell web, just like any other supernatural, but the spell web that covers me is curling around his as well. There's a strange connection I don't understand, but immediately see that I can use to my advantage. I tighten the bond and start to pull his magic away from him, along the spell web, and into my body. I can't hurt him—much—but I can weaken him so I can get away.

He doesn't notice at first, just walks a bit slower. Then he comes to a standstill. "What're you doing to me?" he asks in a whisper.

"I'm sorry. I can't go back there." I manage to push his arm off my back and jump down from his shoulder.

I'm still pulling on his magic, and he slowly turns to look at me. A deep sadness fills his eyes.

"I'm glad you figured out how to get away," he says softly. "I don't want take you back there either."

For a moment, I hesitate. He needs my help, and I want very badly to give it to him. But he shakes his head. "There's nothing you can do for me. Just get outta here fast. There're more coming."

I nod just once and turn away. I've only gone a couple of steps before I turn back to him. "I'll come find you. I'll help you."

He shakes his head slowly. “You can’t do anything for me. But I appreciate it.”

I turn and run to the van, where Amos is in the front seat waiting for me. The engine is running, and Seth is still asleep in the backseat.

“Where did you go to?” Amos’s expression shows his annoyance.

“You didn’t see them? There was a mountain super and another guy.”

Amos stares at me, his eyes wide. “A mountain supernatural?”

I nod. “Can we drive and talk about this?” I’m still holding his power tight to me, but as soon as I let go, the big man is going to come after us. And I have no idea what happened to the other man that I felled so quickly. He must have come to, if Amos didn’t see him.

Amos nods and takes off with a screech of tires.

19

I wake with pain tearing up and down my body. It feels like someone is scratching deep inside with sharp claws. It's all over my skin, as well as deep into the muscle and bone, drawing blood and agony from inside my body.

I scream.

There is no sound, there is no light, just unending pain.

"Mei, wake up!" The voice is familiar, but I'm already awake, so it doesn't help. I arch my body as the claws force their way into my veins.

A hand slaps my cheek and I groan, because I can't manage anything more coherent. A dagger of pain shoves itself into my stomach and I sit bolt upright, eyes wide open and a silent scream erupting out of my mouth.

Arms curl around me, holding me close, lending me healing energy. The pain subsides, and I can breathe again. I slump into the arms and close my eyes. Time seems to stand still, and I lose track of how long I stay like that. Perhaps I doze off, perhaps I don't. After a while, I realize it's Seth who's holding me. The smell of his spicy aftershave combined with that undertone of gunpowder gives him away.

I move slightly, and he lets me go, unwinding his arms. His magic is unusual, like nothing I've ever experienced before. His spell web is patchy, like it can't cover him properly, but it's not because his magic is weak, like I first thought. I frown, trying to figure it out.

"Are you feeling better?" he asks. His voice is soft and gentle. The window lets in the dark night air and the light from a half-moon. I check the clock. It's a few hours since we drove away from the service station.

I nod, unable to speak just yet. I want his arms around me again, but I can't ask. I just stare at him through bruised eyes, my body still trembling.

"What happened?" He looks concerned.

"I... I don't know... I just woke up in pain. Like something was attacking me. I've never felt anything like it." I focus on the clouds crossing over the moon in the sky outside the window. Anything to avoid thinking about the pain.

I paid for two rooms with my credit card, figuring the guys could sleep together. An hour after they reluctantly went to their own room, Seth arrived on my doorstep. "I can't protect you if you're in another room," was all he'd said before bunking down on the floor.

And now, here he is, looking down at me like I'm some fragile flower. I've never been anyone's fragile flower, and I'm not sure I want to start now. Si trained me not to rely on anyone.

I glance down; he has no shirt on. I've just been curled up against those hard muscles and didn't even notice. It takes me a moment to force my eyes back up to his face.

"Is it Vincent?" He's staring hard at me, like I'm a puzzle he needs to solve.

I shake my head. "I don't think so. He's never been able to do anything like that before. And I don't think it's his kind of magic. It's not Earthbound magic."

Seth glances at the wall between my room and theirs. "What about Amos?" he whispers.

I glance toward the room where Amos is sleeping. "He couldn't do it, even if he wanted to. He's practically human." I whisper, as if it's wrong to say it out loud.

Seth doesn't ask how I know.

"Then who is doing this to you?" he says.

"If I knew, I wouldn't be this scared." A chill slithers down my body, and I shiver. Whatever it was, it could happen again at any time.

Seth puts one hand up against my cheek. "We'll figure it out."

I nod shakily. "Sure." I'm not thinking clearly, and I lean forward, dropping my cheek onto his chest. Seth's arms go around me again, and he holds me tight until I fall asleep.

20

When I slowly wake the next morning, I'm curled against something warm. I'm cozy and relaxed, like I've had a good long night's sleep. I hold myself still and keep my eyes closed, unwilling to break the mood. Whatever is out there in the real world can wait.

But the real world doesn't want to wait. Someone starts banging on the door of the room. With a muttered grumble, I turn my face and encounter warm skin. My eyes flick open, and I discover I'm curled up against Seth, who's leaning against the headboard, watching me with his fire-tinted hazel eyes.

I blink and wipe my mouth. Was I drooling? "How...?" I clear my throat. "How long have I been asleep?"

He smiles down at me, clearly amused. "You conked out not long after..." He hesitates. "You needed the sleep."

"You stayed awake all night?"

"I needed to make sure you were okay," he says simply.

"Who's at the door?"

"My guess is that it's the manager to throw us out, or

Amos trying to figure out what we've been doing." He gives a tiny half smile, and his eyes turn from hazel to golden.

"We haven't been doing anything," I say indignantly. Then I blush, remembering his bare chest.

"He doesn't know that."

I pull myself up off of Seth's body and stretch my sore muscles, still ignoring the loud banging on the door. Amos starts calling out. "Mei? Are you okay?"

I sigh and walk over to the door, pulling it open.

His hand is lifted to knock, and his expression is a mix between the kid who feels left out at the party and an annoyed mother hen who can't find one of her chicks. "Are you okay?"

"I'm fine, Amos. I'm probably more able to take care of myself than you are."

He flushes and looks so hurt, it's hard not to feel guilty.

"I'm fine. No baddies here." I sweep an arm back into the room.

He glances into my room. His eyes narrow. "What's Seth doing here?" he asks.

"Seth was just... helping me out," I say, internally wincing as I realize Seth is probably still lying half-naked on my bed. What's he helping me out with? Being naked?

Amos comes into the room, eyeing Seth, who's putting his shirt back on. Thankfully.

"We need to get going," Amos says quietly. I can almost feel the hurt radiating off him.

I harden my resolve. It's not my fault that Amos feels left out. He's a great guy, and he saved our bacon back at the Earthbound compound, but I don't have enough space in my life to pander to him and his hurt feelings. I glance back at Seth. I don't have space for anyone extra in my life right now.

"Okay," I say, trying to keep my voice even. "Sounds good."

"Where are we heading?" Amos asks. "Still east?"

I clear my throat. "I need to take a slight detour. There's a locked box I'd like to pick up." It's occurred to me that this entire situation is exactly the reason Jeff put security boxes in towns around the country.

I need to start making use of them.

And there's one in particular I think Jeff put in place for this exact situation.

Seth immediately shakes his head. "We need to keep to the plan. We have to get to New York as soon as possible."

"It'll take us a couple hours out of the planned trip, and give us clothes, money, and weapons. It's worth the deviation."

"I still say—" Seth tries to argue.

"You're not in charge here," I say, glad for the opportunity to be mad at him. "I'm going, and if you choose not to come, that's fine with me."

Seth stares at me, his eyes flashing cold fire. "Fine."

I try not to miss the warmth that was in his eyes only minutes before.

"I'll go anywhere you want me to," Amos says smugly.

I struggle not to let Amos know how much his answer annoys me as well. "Let's go, then," I say, trying to keep my voice even.

The van starts easily, and we're on the road before we know it, chewing on muesli bars I found in the snack machine. I'm in the front seat, and Seth has settled back into the cushion mattress in the backseat again. He's got his eyes closed as if he's washing himself of this whole business. I know he's just plotting and planning. I can see his spell web, and it's moving busily over his body in that weird patchy way it has.

"So where am I going?" says Amos.

"Quincy, Illinois."

Seth sits up immediately. "No. You *cannot* go there, Mei. They know about that place. Even *I* know about that place."

I shake my head. "They don't know for certain we'll go there."

"They can guess. Both the SIG and the Earthbound know you've got ties to that town. You can't risk it."

"If it makes you feel better, we could contact the SIG and tell them we'll meet some agents there."

"You know as well as I do how the Earthbound found you. That tracker inside me didn't just appear. There's a traitor at the SIG."

Amos flicks a startled glance in my direction, and I take a breath. I had an idea Seth was going to argue. But I also know that I have to do this before going to see my father and the SIG. "It's important Seth. Otherwise I wouldn't be doing it."

"They'll know it's a place you might go. That you feel at home there. There will be people waiting for you. It'll be impossible to escape a second time."

"Nothing's impossible," I murmur to myself. It's the echo of an argument that Si and I always used to have. He'd make me do something difficult, I'd argue the point, and he'd always make me do it anyway.

"That's nonsense. Some things *are* impossible. You can't win every time. Si and Jeff's deaths are an example of that, Mei. Listen to me on this. If you go to Quincy, you'll be caught."

I'm silent a moment, thinking through Seth's arguments. I don't want to go back to the Earthbound. I twitch every time I think about the fire pit and the glass water chamber. But there's a part of me that's positive I need to go. Despite the challenges, despite every reason why I know I shouldn't.

It all comes down to Jeff.

There was a riddle that Jeff always used to quote to me, and the answer was Quincy. One time he made me solve this mind-bendingly cryptic crossword, and the solution was Quincy. Another time he made up a trivia game, where all the answers ended up being Quincy. It got to the point where I would just answer 'Quincy' when he gave me something hard to do, just in case it was the answer.

This morning I woke up convinced he was preparing me for this moment. So... "I'm going, and you can't stop me."

Seth falls silent, and I can see he's brooding over it. Maybe considering if he can overpower me. Force me to go straight to my father.

Next to me, Amos seems happy for the first time since we left the Earthbound facility, humming under his breath. I have a strong suspicion it's because Seth and I are fighting.

We get to a roadside diner just outside of Jefferson City for our evening meal. Amos has been chatting to me as if we're on the college road trip he so desperately wanted. Seth has been sleeping for most of the day and hasn't spoken to either of us. I shake his arm to wake him up, and he simply opens his eyes. He's as clear as a bell. He hasn't been asleep at all, at least not recently.

"Don't you try anything," I whisper. "I'm doing this."

"You'll get caught. Do you really want that?"

"I can do it. I *have* to do it. Jeff told me to do it. I just didn't remember about it till now."

Seth shakes his head and gently pulls his arm away from my hand. I sigh and step away from the door of the van. "We're eating here. Then we'll find a motel for the night."

We eat in silence, and I keep waiting for Seth to make his move. I know he's planning something, and it will have to involve holding me hostage. I don't know how I feel about that. At least he's doing it because he's trying to keep me safe.

Amos isn't oblivious, but he's not above using the silence to charm me. And if it had been a normal day, in a normal life, perhaps he could have charmed me. Amos is an attractive guy. There's no denying that. He's got chocolate-brown eyes and smooth skin with a touch of warmth to it. When you add in his shaggy black hair, he reminds me of one of those slightly too intense college guys who likes to talk about philosophy and how to make the world a better place. His smile is adorable, and when he's on form, he's got a measure of his father's charisma.

Sure, on a normal day, in a normal world, maybe I could fall for someone like Amos.

But I'm not normal, and never have been.

I don't live in a normal world, and right now, I don't have time for that kind of shit. I'm going to get the damned locked box in Quincy whether I have one or none or both of them with me.

21

He waits so long to make his move, I almost think I'm wrong.

It's the middle of the night, we're in another dodgy motel, this time all sharing a room with three single beds. I figured it was easier than putting up with another late-night visit from Seth insisting he needed to protect me.

Who knows what I might consider letting him do.

I sense rather than see him get out of his bed. He creeps past Amos, who is sleeping on the middle single bed, and comes to stand at the end of my bed. His spell web is crackling with energy, the most I've ever seen running across his grid. It leaps and pulls at the broken strands, almost like it's trying to heal itself. I'm mesmerized for a moment, until I realize this is it. He's going to try and stop me.

I move restlessly, pretending it's in my sleep, to get into a better position to see what he's going to do.

Before I can move, Amos leaps out of his bed and hits Seth over the head with a frying pan from the small motel kitchen. Seth falls forward onto my bed, unconscious.

I open my mouth to scream, the sudden violence shocking me more than it should. I reach out to touch Seth's spell web, making sure he's okay. He's unconscious, but it will take more than a whack from Amos to kill him.

"Come on. Let's go. We can leave him here. He doesn't want to go to Quincy with us." Amos is standing with the frying pan over his shoulder like it's a weapon.

I hesitate. But I know it's for the best. Seth didn't want to go to Quincy, and Amos is going to take me. I can't keep watching out for Seth to make his move, even if he's doing it with good intentions.

I climb out of bed and pull Seth up a bit so his head is resting on the pillow. His face looks serene, like he's just fallen asleep, not been knocked unconscious. He groans softly and I jump back. I glance at Amos, and he gestures for me to hurry. We need to get out of here.

I race off down the hallway, following Amos. We're in the van and backing out onto the street when I see Seth emerge from our room. Part of me is relieved that he's able to stand so soon after that knock. He watches as we speed off down the street, the night lights the only thing showing the way.

"Do you think he'll be angry?"

"You betcha." Amos can't hide his grin.

I nod. He's right. Of course Seth will be pissed. I try to steel myself to the idea of an angry Seth instead of the gentle Seth who looked after me when I was in pain. Have I done the right thing? I glance at Amos. I don't think he'd hurt me. He's determined to help me do everything I want, in fact.

"Why are you sticking around, Amos?" I ask. "I mean, it's not your fight, is it?"

He glances at me, his face turning serious. "It's because

of you, Mei." He hesitates. "It's going to sound dumb, but it's like there's a light that shines from your eyes. It makes me want to follow you to the ends of the Earth." His voice is soft but intense. He means everything he's saying.

I clear my throat. It suddenly feels ten degrees hotter in the van. "We can never be more than friends, you understand that?" I say carefully.

"If this about my father—"

I shake my head. "My life is complicated. I don't have room for anyone else."

"You're not even giving us a chance." Amos's voice is tight with suppressed emotion.

"Maybe if we'd met in a different time and place," I say, trying to let him down gently. I see immediately that it's a mistake. His face lights up again.

"So when this is all over, we can be together?"

My lips harden into a thin line. Anger boils below the surface. "When do you think it's ever going to be *over* for me?" I say, the words whipping out of my mouth. "Your father is going to hunt me for the rest of my life, do you understand that? One day he might even succeed in capturing me again, and then he's going to torture me on the pretext of proving I'm a dragon." The words just spill out, but I can't help myself, he's just so naïve. "Do you know the worst thing? It's that he's going to realize he was wrong—as soon as I'm dead."

"I don't... He's not..." Amos can't find the words to defend his father. His expression is stricken, and I can tell he doesn't know how to deal with my accusations.

"Let's not talk about it anymore, okay? I'm tired. Wake me for my driving shift in an hour." I curl up against the window and pretend to sleep. In reality I stare out into the dark night and watch the street lights whip past the window.

Amos keeps driving, heading out of the city and onto the highway. The van is still running smoothly, despite the miles we've been clocking up. Neither of us speaks for a long time, both caught up in our own thoughts. I'm trying to remember everything about Quincy that I can. I've stayed there a total of three times, but it's one of the places we were ambushed by the Earthbound.

In spectacular style.

As in they took out half the town, over one hundred humans died, and the SIG had to make up a fake explosion at a local factory and cast a massive amnesia spell to account for it to the humans.

It's also where Lee was killed.

I'm not planning on going anywhere near where it happened. I'm more interested in figuring out where Jeff would have hidden the information I'm now convinced he's left there. I need to find out what's real and what's not about this whole situation. If I'm not the dragon, then who is? How did they convince the Earthbound that I was the baby they were looking for? My whole life makes no sense. I need some answers, and I'm convinced Jeff has left them for me in Quincy.

Minutes slide into hours as the darkness drifts past my window. We pull over to switch drivers. Amos goes to the toilet and grabs something to eat at an all-night Seven Eleven, while I wait impatiently in the car. "I'll drive until we're just outside of Quincy," I say. "I think I need to be on guard once we get there."

Amos nods, his face pensive, and a while later when I see the outskirts of Quincy through the lightening sky, I slow the van to a stop at the side of the road. So soon. I shudder.

Amos gets into the driver's seat, but doesn't drive off. "Where to?" he asks staring out the windscreen at the small town in front of us. He taps his forefinger on the steering wheel nervously. I understand why he's anxious. I'm leading him into what could be an extremely dangerous situation. I have butterflies in my stomach too.

"We should head to Bicentennial Park, by the river," I say. I'm not entirely sure why I say it, because where I need to go is West Quincy. I've figured out where Jeff would have left information for me. But I've been taught too well by my mentor. *Never reveal yourself too soon*, he would say, *it'll just come back to bite you on the arse*. I'm sure I can trust Amos; I just need him to prove it to me.

When we arrive at the park, I climb out of the van and stand at the edge of the grass. It's starting to spit tiny drops of rain, more like a mist really. The sun is emerging from the east, casting a glowing morning light over the water of the Mississippi River and the bridges on either side of the park.

I walk to the gazebo and turn my face to the sun. As it comes up over the edge of the landscape, a rainbow appears, drawn by the perfect mix of light rain and early morning sun. I take a deep breath, trying to memorize the feeling, to link it to a time years ago when I lived here.

I need a moment of peace, and this place always gave that to me. Lee and I used to run along the edges of the river on clear early mornings just like this one. We would chat about everything, from the latest current events to our favorite television programs. I can almost hear him laughing as I tell a funny story. The memory is so strong I don't immediately notice the SUV pulling up, or hear the helicopter in the sky above us.

"I'm sorry, Mei. This is just too important," Amos says behind me.

I blink, turning toward him. "What?"

He's holding a handgun pointed at me and looks above us to where a helicopter is circling in the rain. "I'll make sure my father takes better care of you this time. He won't hurt you like he did before."

22

It takes me a few seconds to comprehend what he's done.

I glance at the SUV, the helicopter, and then back at Amos. The rain is getting heavier, making puddles in the concrete paths around the gazebo. "But you helped me escape," I whisper, taking a step toward him, holding one hand out.

Something flashes in his eyes, gone too fast for me to decipher. "I thought I was doing the right thing. I thought you were...different."

A terrible feeling swirls inside my stomach. "Is this because of our conversation last night?" I ask, my hands tightening into fists.

Amos takes a small step back. "Of course not. I just..." He looks away, his face flushed. "I talked to my father, and he made me see sense."

I can't believe he's done this. "I can't go back there, Amos," I whisper. His gun wavers, and Amos points it to the ground.

I let out a breath. "You know what he did to me," I add. Just a little closer and I'll be able to get the gun.

"This is bigger than you or me," he says, and pushes his other hand through his unruly hair. "This is about the survival of the whole world." I can almost hear his father saying the words to him.

Tears well in my eyes. "I'm not a dragon, Amos."

At my words, he jerks the gun up to point at my chest again. "My father told me what happened in the furnace. He said the temperatures were up to two hundred degrees Fahrenheit, and you didn't even blink. That the stones you pulled up from the floor of the furnace were even hotter, and you pulled them up with your bare hands. No one can do that." Rain on the roof of the gazebo provides a dramatic backdrop for his words.

A panicky feeling rises inside me. I shake my head. "That's not true, Amos. Your father is just telling you that so he can force me to go back there. He's wrong."

"My father is many things, but he's not a liar. He sees no point."

"The way he sees the world isn't the way it is," I say desperately. The helicopter is landing in the open space next to the gazebo, and I acknowledge that it's my own fault for bringing Amos here.

"I thought I could trust you," I whisper. I should have known that there's no one I can trust but myself. Not any more.

Amos winces, but says nothing. There's nothing he can say.

On the heels of acceptance comes anger. Who does he think he is? Why do the Earthbound insist on following me around, treating me like a commodity they need to acquire?

Even Amos, who believes he has feelings for me, doesn't see that it's wrong. "This isn't what's best for everyone," I say, still trying to make him see reason. Or at least my point of view.

"My father is a great man. He's doing what is best for the world, for all of us." His eyes are glowing in the early morning light. "Not everyone has to strength of will to actually do that." Amos believes what he's saying, and that makes me really, really mad.

"You'll have to tie me down somewhere deep inside your fortress if you think you're going to keep me there," I say, my voice sneering at him. "I will never help your father." The thought of chains around my wrists and ankles makes me tremble. Sweat runs in thick rivulets down my body. I'll be at their mercy again. My whole being rebels against the idea. Anger rolls off me in waves, and sparks hiss inside me. A burning rage pushes itself up from my center and I struggle to keep the heat under control. Thunder rumbles somewhere nearby.

I need to be cool and calm if I'm going to get out of this. I know that with every fiber of my being. Si instilled that in me from the very first moment I started learning the Protectors' fighting style. Cool and calm will win every fight. But the heat is too much and it rises uncontrollably up my body, until I feel like I'm on fire. I'm hotter than I ever felt inside Vincent's damned furnace.

The helicopter lands on the grass near the gazebo. I'm frozen like a rabbit in the headlights, unable to save myself. I'm sure there is something I could do, but my brain won't help me. I'm going to be taken by the Earthbound. Kept like a pet, routinely tested on. Perhaps they'll eventually figure out I'm not a dragon, but I doubt it; at least not before they kill me.

I fling my arm out toward the helicopter, toward the enemy, as if I can push them away. Lightning flashes in the sky above me, and a jagged line of electrical light hits my body. Sparks explode around the gazebo. Instead of burning me up, the lightning escapes along my arm, travelling across the park and slamming into the helicopter in a burst of fiery energy. It explodes in a giant ball of flames, pieces of metal flying into the air. Whoever is in the helicopter is now ashes.

Some of the debris hits the SUV, breaking the windscreen and denting the doors. Two men dive out of the vehicle and run from the flames.

I watch the seething mass of fire for a second, too stunned to move. Then pain rises up through my chest, the same unstoppable clawing agony from the other night, and I crumple to the ground, putting my hands to my head, trying to stop whatever is attacking me from the inside. My skin and bone are being torn apart and I can't stop it. I hear someone screaming, and then realize it's me. The pain doesn't stop and I can't think past it.

Hands grab my arms, and I shake them off. I'll never go with them. I'd rather die.

"Mei, it's Seth. Don't fight me."

It takes a few moments before I understand the words. "I... the pain..." is all I can manage to mumble.

"Is it like the other night?" he asks.

I nod.

"We have to get to the water. I knocked out Amos, but the police will turn up soon. We can't explain a blown-up helicopter."

I nod again. "Let's go," I whisper, barely able to put the two words together.

Seth has to drag me to the boat ramp beside the gazebo through the pouring rain. There's a heavy slanting wall of water beating down on us from the heavens now. I can hardly see where we're going, but we cross the park and into the water almost before I realize it.

I stumble deeper into the river and the water surrounds my body, allowing its energy to mingle with mine. The pain dies off, and I'm able to focus on what's happening for the first time since Amos pulled the gun on me.

Seth pulls me along in the water, and after a while, I start to use my arms and legs to help him. The water is flowing swiftly, the rain making the currents stronger than usual.

Soon enough, my strength returns, and I pull away, able to swim for myself. Seth grabs onto an overhanging branch under the bridge and waits for me, treading water. I grasp his arm as I move by and swing into the side of the river next to him.

"How did you find us?" I ask, holding the branch to one side of him.

"I knew where you were going." Seth shrugs. His eyes are dark and unreadable in the shadows of the bridge. "And I put a locator beacon on the van, just in case."

"Where did you get—" I start to ask. But then I think about Jeff and what he would have done. "You had them on you the whole time?" I ask.

Seth nods.

Jeff always carried useful items, including locator beacons, sewn into his clothing. Supernatural technology had made them small enough to carry and potent enough to use. This is the first time it occurs to me that it might be SIG policy, rather than Jeff's paranoia.

But it doesn't really matter how he found me. "Thank you," I say, and grab him in a tight waterlogged hug. Just that he did.

After a moment's hesitation, he puts his arm around me and hugs me back.

23

We swim in the shallows, trying to keep out of the deep, swift current of the Mississippi River. The rain helps to cover our tracks and keep us hidden.

I follow Seth, and after a while, once we're a decent distance down the river, I drag myself up the bank after him. He leans down and pulls me up the rest of the way and we stumble along the backstreets to where Seth parked the car he stole from the motel. He's as paranoid as I am.

Except I wasn't paranoid enough.

I don't say anything until we're in the car and Seth is looking at me expectantly. "Where to?" he asks.

I look into his fiery hazel eyes and hesitate. He's as steady as Si or Jeff. He's been with me through thick and thin; been shot, kidnapped, and hit over the head, and he's never once deserted me. Fear curls in my stomach. *I thought I could trust Amos, too.*

I close my eyes and take a deep breath. I know in my gut that Seth can be trusted. I never felt that way with Amos. "It's at the pawnshop in West Quincy," I whisper. Without a word, he turns the ignition, puts the car in gear, and we head off.

I don't know how he knows his way around Quincy. I suspect I don't want to know, especially if it's got anything to do with me. We cross the bridge, and I stare through the rain down at the Mississippi River below us, my clothes still wet from its sluggish brown waters. The water surges past, the storm making its murky depths run faster than usual.

I glance back at the smoking remains of the helicopter. At least the rain has stopped the fire from spreading. I can just see the outlines of police cars and fire engines there now, with men in uniforms circling the area. A figure that looks like Amos is being questioned by police inside the gazebo. His shoulders are slumped and he keeps glancing into the sky as if expecting another helicopter.

Ahead of us—across the other side of the bridge—is West Quincy, a whole other state and a whole other problem. I'm sure Jeff meant me to do this, but I'm not sure why, and I'm scared. I can acknowledge that to myself as I sit huddled in the passenger seat next to Seth.

The pawnshop is a place I've only visited once before with Jeff. I didn't get it at the time, and I'm not sure I get it now. It was just before Lee was killed, and Jeff pawned a locked wooden box with strange patterns and metal corners and locks.

I don't know if the box will still be there. In fact, logic states that it won't be. But I have this feeling I'm going to find it hidden away in the backroom somewhere, just waiting for me.

My hands tremble at the thought of touching something that Jeff had put together so long ago. What if there's a note from him in there? It will be like he's come back from the grave. I don't know if I can handle that.

I let out a breath.

The truth is, I have no idea what's in there, and I can't worry about it. In five minutes' time, I'll have all the answers to my questions. Who am I? Who is the real dragon?

Am I really just a decoy?

I glance back at the smoking helicopter, then down at my hands. If I'm a dragon, I *will* eat my hat. But something is going on that I need to understand. I've been kept in the dark far too long. My twentieth birthday is fast approaching.

Seth parks in front of the West Quincy Pawnshop. It's just a small shop in a bigger white wooden building with a corrugated iron roof. There's a green awning over the green front door.

We run out into the rain again, and I push open the door, peering into the darkened interior. Seth follows me and we both take it in slowly. There's stuff everywhere. Shelves and shelves of stuff, musical instruments, pictures, bikes, lamps, glass cases with jewelry, drawers with who knows what inside them, guns at the back behind a locked cabinet door. There's even a motorbike in the back corner.

"What are we looking for?" Seth asks.

"A patterned wooden box, about this big." I hold my hands out, trying to indicate the foot-long box with my hands.

He nods and heads off, digging in and around the back of the store. I wander around, trying to remember if this is what it was like when I was younger. I don't think so. It seems more organized now, more clinical. More professional probably. I try to let my instincts guide me, but all I can think about is how my damp pants are rubbing against the inside of my legs.

I spot some clothes in the corner, and resolve to buy something new to wear. I'm holding up a pair of jeans when an old man appears beside me. I jerk backward, surprise making my heart pound. He's stooped over, with a lined face and mismatched clothes.

"Can I help you, ma'am?" he says, his pale blue eyes boring into me. He's covered by the spell web, and is looking at me like he knows me.

"Uh... I thought... I want to try this on." I look around for Seth, but he's at the other end of the store.

Blue eyes flash. "Are you sure that's all?"

"A box," I blurt. "I'm looking for a wooden box."

He nods, and his eyes glow for a second. "That's what I thought. As soon as I saw you, I knew you were here for the box."

"You have it?" I say, hardly able to believe my luck.

"I do. It's out the back, where we keep all our... special... items."

I glance around again, looking for Seth, but I can't see him. Where could he have gone?

"Come with me. I'll show it to you." He gestures toward a red curtain hanging behind the counter. I hesitate, but this is what I've come here for. I have to go get it.

He holds the curtain to one side and I duck my head going through. It's dark, lit only by a single dirty lamp that gives off a hazy glow.

"If you come this way, I'll show you the special room where we keep our most valuable items."

Again I hesitate. I should have told Seth where I was going. I glance back out to the main shop.

"Don't worry, your friend will be fine."

He reaches out with one gnarled hand and turns the brass handle of an old carved wooden door. It opens inward, and he enters ahead of me, holding the door open as I cautiously follow him into the space.

It's a magical version of the pawnshop outside. Artifacts, talismans, objects of power, cards—everything you could possibly wish to own or hold as a magic user. The room is dark, with only narrow dirty windows at the top of the room letting in light. The rain is beating on the roof, making the room feel even smaller.

I take another step inside and then another. Several objects call out to me, whispers of energy that I want to answer.

"Watch yourself. There are objects that are... less than savory. You wouldn't want to get yourself caught by one of them."

I glance at him; his face is showing an unholy amusement. I don't think he'd be bothered if I got sucked into one of these objects of power. He's the kind of person who might have a bit of a chuckle about it and then go back to eating his cheese sandwich out in the main store.

"It's over there in the corner."

I follow his pointed finger, and there it is, just as I remember it. Well, almost. It's smaller and less polished. But it's definitely the one Jeff left here. I tiptoe carefully around the worst of the objects, the ones with the strongest pull. The spell web coats all the objects as well, something I've never seen before. They must have sufficient power to kick it into gear. It's this whisper of a thought that makes me look up again. He's a collector of powerful magic objects. He's not going to let one go, just because I came back and asked for it.

Turning, I bounce a couple of times, reminding myself to be light on my feet. He's right behind me, with a small blue bottle raised in my direction. A strange blue mist is seeping out the slim bottle neck, and I immediately step back as fast as I can, trying not to breathe in any of the mist.

"What are you doing?" I say.

"There's a bounty on your head. I can't let an opportunity like that go by."

I remember the radio announcement Vincent put up before he captured me. "That was for the humans. It wasn't a supernatural bounty."

"It's been upgraded. The Earthbound are very anxious to get hold of you. I'm just doing my civic duty."

"Civic duty my ass. You're doing this for the money. Whatever they're offering, I'll pay more," I say desperately.

"They're offering one million dollars." He raises his eyebrows at me. "Care to beat that offer?"

My eyes bug out at the amount. "Seriously?" Anger burns for a moment. "What the hell? Why doesn't he just give up?" I glare at the old man. I don't have that kind of cash lying around. "I'll talk to the SIG. They'll pay it for me."

He laughs. "They won't pay a dime."

"Do you know what they think I am?" I ask.

He shakes his head. "Must be pretty special, based on the reward." He shrugs. "I don't care."

"The last of the dragons." I hold up one hand and a flame appears over my fingers. It's just a small piece of magic, easy for most supers, but perhaps it will work on the old man, whatever he is. I can't tell what kind of magic he has, other than he's a supernatural.

He steps closer, and this time his eyes are glowing a bright frosty blue, like he's got torches shining out from behind his irises. It matches the color of the mist coming out of the bottle.

I see immediately that I've made a serious tactical error.

"I've never had a dragon in my collection," he says with a luminous smile.

24

"You never intended to give me the box, did you?" I say, trying to stall.

Taking a step backward, I try to figure out what I can use in the room around me. There are lots of items, just not any I'm prepared to actually touch. They all have dark and painful vibrations coming from them, and I know nothing good will come from manhandling them.

"The box is mine now. You took too long before coming back. Your SIG agent should have known better than to leave it so long with me."

His eyes glow brighter for a second and I shiver. He must be some kind of water elemental; living next to the Mississippi, it would make sense.

"Bullshit," I say, stepping behind a table set up with various knives. I'm tempted to pick one up, but the spell web is buckling and shifting over them in such an unstable way, I know I'd regret it.

My best bet is to avoid touching any of the terrible artifacts surrounding me.

"Is there anything in here not full of darkness and hate?"

I ask caustically. I'm trying to distract him, but I'm interested in the answer.

"My collection is varied. I have everything I could possibly desire in here."

Not much of an answer. But I know the answer for myself, I can see it through the spell web. "I'll buy the box off you."

He scoffs. "Well of course, you would have done that. But now I know what you are, I think I would prefer you in my collection."

My heart skids to a halt. I've done this to myself, I know that. "I'm *not* a dragon. They just think I am. I was trying to scare you."

He looks me up and down. "I admit, you don't look like a dragon."

Something pings inside me, and I realize I'm insulted. "What does a dragon look like then?"

"Bigger perhaps? More intimidating?"

My eyes narrow. "Intimidation is overrated." I make a dash for the box in the corner, grab it, and back off before he can make a move. I admit to myself that I was trying to show off my speed.

And it works. Dammit.

He's staring at me with a collector's expression; an otherworldly greed mixed with a single-minded focus on getting what he wants. "It doesn't matter whether you're a dragon or not. I've decided to add you to my collection. You have an interesting mix of talents." He takes a step toward me and holds up the smoking bottle. "The spell in this bottle is too powerful, even for a dragon." He smiles, and I see a row of pointy brown teeth.

The blue smoke wafts toward me and I feel the strong seduction of the magic. It's like a magnet that's been tuned to me personally. I can't let it touch me, or it'll be the end. Or at least the end of me living *outside* the little blue bottle.

The spell web shudders as the smoke drifts over it, and I send a wave of energy along the grid. The smoke hesitates, then continues floating toward me. Taking a step back, I bump into another table, disturbing a row of tiny bottles.

One falls to the floor and crashes wide open. I jerk back and the strange man in front of me swears. The wooden box slips to one side under my arm, and I grasp it more tightly.

Holding my breath, I steady myself to fend off whatever magic was caught inside the broken bottle. Something emerges, a blurry outline of a dark creature. It issues a low growl and pauses near me; I tense, unsure if it's a threat. But after a second of hesitation, it simply escapes out of the room through the ceiling vents as fast as it can go.

It wasn't interested in me, just in getting out of the room.

How many of the other magical objects in this room feel the same way? Letting the creatures escape might provide me with the distraction I need. It can't be a worse plan than allowing that blue mist to suck me into the bottle for God knows how many years.

I'm not going to be a damn genie.

Swiping at the rest of the vials on the tabletop, I knock them all to the floor.

They break open on contact with the hard concrete, and I step back and away as mist and smoke burst forth from the remains. None stay around to chat, but the action has distracted the old man enough for me to make a few steps around to the other side of the room. I see another couple of bottles, bigger ones this time, on a shelf near me. I turn and lift a hand to swipe them down to the floor, between me and the old man.

"No!" he yells. "Not that one!" He tries to leap for me, but he's too slow and old.

Like I'm going to listen to him, anyway.

The bottles make a satisfying crash onto the floor, and break in two, exactly at halfway.

It's strange after the chaos of the vials to see such precision.

This time the smoke is slow to emerge, and before too much escapes, I know I've made a terrible mistake. I back up toward the door as a creature solidifies out of the smoke and into real life. He's big and muscled and vaguely human-shaped, but looks like he's just escaped from the depths of a fire, with smoke and soot and ash covering his body. Flames burst out from pockets on his skin, and his hair is more flame than anything else. He's a demon.

Turns out my tormentor was right. I should have left that one alone.

The demon swipes at me with one large meaty fist, but he's slow, still getting his bearings from being in the bottle, and I manage to leap out of the way. I look left and right, trying to find something that might help. Fire won't affect him, but something to cool him down? I spot a fridge in the corner of the room and feel the ice sitting inside just waiting for me to use it.

But before I can figure out a plan, the demon pauses and sniffs the air. He turns toward the back of the room, like he's hunting something down.

The pawnshop owner is cowering in one corner, his hands over his head, repeating some kind of protection spell over and over. It's the kind of useless spell that doesn't even provide a blip on the spell web, and I hesitate for a moment, looking at the door behind me. I could leave right now, let the shop owner take what he's got coming and get out.

But then I look at the demon, twice the size of anything I've seen before, and I know I can't let it loose on the world. I have to clean up my mess.

"Hey, ugly!" I yell, trying to get his attention. He clearly isn't that bothered by name calling, because he ignores me and continues toward his prey. I'm pretty sure I'm next, as soon as he's torn his tormentor limb from limb.

Putting the wooden box down by the carved wooden door, I race to the fridge and open it, trying to gauge what I have to work with.

Using my water magic, I pull the ice out, elongating it into long, thin spikes. I hold a dozen of them in the air, aimed at the demon, and flick my wrist, sending them at top speed toward the fire-covered creature. They enter his skin and immediately melt in a sizzling hiss of steam. The demon roars, holding his head back like he's a wolf baying at the moon.

And then he lowers his head and turns to look at me. There's such heat and hatred in his gaze, I can barely keep looking at him. He's making a promise to me, I know that much. Then he turns back to the pawnshop owner. He makes one final leap and lands on top of the man. Long claws rake the man's body, separating skin from bone.

Swallowing down the bile that's burning my throat at the sight, I leap onto the demon's back and force my arms around its neck. Pulling them closed, I try to block off its air. It occurs to me too late that a demon probably doesn't need to breathe.

It shakes me off like a rag doll and throws me across the room. I smash into the wall beside the carved door and drop down to land on a small coffee table laden with dolls and toys. My back feels like I've been run over by a train, and I think my head might be bleeding.

I see stars for a couple of minutes as I try to figure out what just happened.

At least now I know that demons don't breathe.

Something is digging into my side and I pull out a small toy train. I drop it immediately when the dark energy coming off it tries to soak into my skin.

Across the room, there is silence except for the wet sounds of the demon eating raw meat. For a moment, I consider vomiting, but don't have time or the energy.

The demon will turn to me next.

25

A fist pounding on the outside door distracts me.

Seth.

He's yelling my name, and in the next second, something crashes against the locked door. He's trying to smash it in.

I need to finish this off fast, or he's going to get killed as well.

I pull myself to my feet, even as the demon stands up on its hind legs. Blood is dripping from its mouth, and when it grins at me, I see pieces of raw flesh stuck between its sharpened teeth.

It advances slowly, and I try to think straight. The wooden box at my feet catches my eye, and I grab it in both hands. Maybe this isn't quite what Jeff had in mind as a use for the box, but if it helps me get out of this mess, I'll take it. When it's close enough, I take a running leap forward, holding the wooden box high. I only have one shot, so I have to get it right.

It's such an unexpected move that I manage to slam the box into the side of the demon's head and then leap to one side. It halts, and rusty-red demon blood gushes down its face from the wound. But it just grins and slaps me with one meaty fist. The blast of its blow knocks me to the ground, and my head slams against the concrete. Dazed, I look up at the demon looming over me. I try to pull myself backward along the floor. A whimpering noise comes from my mouth, and I wish I could make myself shut the hell up.

What I need is a plan, not scaredy-cat noises.

But no plans magically appear in my head, just a roaring noise that blocks everything else out.

The roaring becomes louder and louder until I can't hear anything else. The demon is so close I can feel its heat on my face. I open my mouth to scream and the roaring erupts from my mouth like molten lava from a volcano.

The sound waves knock the demon backward. I sit up and open my mouth again. Another roar bursts out, shoving the demon across the room, crashing it into a shelf full of weapons. Knives, swords, and other more obscure weapons rain down on the demon, some of them cutting open its skin.

He's lying next to the mangled remains of the shop owner, and I have to concentrate really hard on not gagging at the sight. The smell of blood and magic lies heavy across the room.

Something blue catches my eye.

Lying near the old man's body is the little blue bottle he'd been trying to trap me in. The cork stopper at the top has been replaced; he must have decided to save it for after the demon attack. He was obviously a glass-half-full kind of guy.

I surge forward and grab the tiny bottle.

Without thinking, I lift one arm and pull on the demon through the spell web. It's still dazed and its eyes aren't focused, but it moves toward me. It growls, low and deep. The noise sends shivers down my spine. Its eyes start to clear. I wonder if I really want it closer to me.

I lift my hand again, but this time, energy buzzing in the air over my head makes me pause. I hear the boom of thunder overhead. Moments later, a streak of lightning bursts through the metal roof of the old building, straight into my hand. It ricochets out from my hand and into the demon.

I squeeze my eyes closed, trying to block out the mind-blowing energy that's hurtling around the small room. There's a sizzling, burning sound, and a flash of bright light. And then it's quiet. I open my eyes, and the demon is lying beside me, its fires out and its eyes closed. I poke at its body with one foot. It's not moving.

I don't think demons can die. I'm pretty sure about this fact. But this one has been knocked out for the count. I uncork the bottle and hold it out in front of me with both hands. The blue smoke emerges again and I can only hope that it's not going to trap me in there instead of the demon. My heart is beating one hundred miles an hour, and sweat drips down my back. I've never done anything like this before, and it's only because the demon came from another bottle that it occurs to me it's even possible.

The smoke hesitates, and I hold my breath. Then it locks onto the demon, wafting in its direction.

Even unconscious, it resists, straining against the magic in the bottle. But it's been locked away a long time and it's taken out most of its initial rage on the pawnshop owner. The blue mist touches its legs, and they start to shrink, even as they're pulled toward the bottle. I feel a moment of remorse—I'd be angry too if I'd been locked in a bottle for who-knows-how long. Its rage doesn't mean it deserves to go back into another prison. Then I remember the likely consequences of setting it free. I glance over at the pile of gore that was once a strange old man.

The pawnshop owner brought it on himself by trying to lock me up in a damn bottle and keeping dangerous demons in his basement. But the people who will be affected by this demon are all around me, innocents living their daily lives without knowledge of the supernatural, and I have no intention of letting them suffer for my moment of weakness.

A loud, splintering noise comes from the doorway, and the door breaks in half. Seth bursts through the shattered remains, his face red from the exertion. He glances around the disordered room, his eyes pausing on the half-eaten body of the owner and then flicking to me.

I'm still trying to hold the blue bottle out as far away from me as I can. The upper body and arms of the demon are being sucked through the tiny neck of the bottle. With a pop, the demon's head squeezes down the narrow opening and I screw the top over it.

Seth walks cautiously over to me. "Are you okay?"

I lift the tiny bottle, which now has a moving cloud of dark energy flowing across its surface. "I think so," I whisper. I put the bottle in my pocket, then reach one hand to my head and feel the blood matted in with the hair.

"What the hell happened? I heard the sound of fighting."

I blink. What *did* happen? "He tried to collect me," I say, gesturing to the old man.

Seth frowns down at the owner's body; it's already starting to smell.

"He's rotting faster than he should," Seth notes. "I think we should get out of here. Fast."

I just nod. He takes my hand, and I realize I'm still trembling.

As we walk past the door, I stop, trying to pick up Jeff's wooden box, now covered in demon blood. The rusty orange color stands out against the intricate patterns on the wood. Seth pushes my hand aside and picks it up in one large hand. He tucks it under his arm and pulls me out of the room.

Running back out into the anteroom and through the pawn store, we emerge into the daylight outside. The rain has stopped and now the sun is shining over everything, making it sparkle with reflected light.

I stop and suck in a deep breath of fresh air. The little blue bottle feels heavy in my pocket.

"We need to get the hell out of here before someone sees us." Seth pulls on my hand.

I nod and take another deep breath. Then I let him drag me back to the small stolen car. He unlocks my door without a word and helps me into the passenger seat.

We're in the car and driving away from Quincy before he speaks again.

"Did you get what you came for?" He's eyeing the bloodied wooden box that I have clutched to my chest.

I nod.

"Tell me what happened in there."

I shake my head. "Drive. Just drive," I whisper.

26

We've been driving for an hour before I feel okay enough to whisper, "I'm sorry."

Seth glances at me, and then back at the road. He doesn't say anything for a while. Then: "For what?"

"For leaving you like that. It was dumb."

"Why did you do it?"

I shrug. "You were planning to kidnap me. Force me to go with you."

Seth shakes his head. "No, I wasn't. I didn't agree, but I wouldn't have stopped you."

I try to think back, to remember why I was so certain. "Then why did you get up? Why were you standing over me?"

A red flush works its way over Seth's face. "I wasn't going to hurt you. I just couldn't sleep." He pauses. "Did you plan it with Amos? Hitting me over the head?"

I shake my head, too embarrassed by the idea that I trusted Amos to speak.

"When did you find out he had double-crossed us?" he asks quietly.

"Not until he pulled the gun on me," I say, gazing out the window. "Even then, I thought I could convince him to change his mind."

"Why did he do it? Did he say?" Seth asks softly.

I hesitate. I'm convinced Amos was feeling hurt and rejected when he phoned his father, which made him vulnerable to Vincent's persuasion. He must have done it when we stopped to switch drivers on the way to Quincy.

But is that really why he turned on me? Or is it because of the bigger picture? Amos grew up with the Earthbound, he believes in what they're doing. Perhaps this was always the way it was going to end, no matter what Amos thought when he first helped me.

I mull over what Vincent told Amos. Was it true? I didn't think so when Amos first said the words, but now... Too many strange things are happening around me.

I bite my lip, still not sure what to say. Do I even want Seth to know everything? The one thing I learned from Amos is that I shouldn't trust anyone.

But Seth... He's stuck with me through all of this. He's never complained about being on the run, getting shot, almost being killed; he's never given up on me. I take a breath. "He said the furnace they put me in at the Earthbound headquarters was really hot. Far too hot for a normal supernatural to survive. He still thinks I'm a dragon." I haven't said those words out loud before, and a shiver of emotion rolls down my body.

"Wait. What?" Seth puts his foot on the brake and skids to a stop on the side of the narrow country road we're driving along. "They put you in a furnace?"

My hands are clenched in my lap. I hadn't told him what they did to me up til now. I take a breath and the words flow out, difficult at first, but soon tripping over themselves. I tell him everything. As I talk, Seth's expression tightens with anger.

When I'm finished, he doesn't speak for a while, just leans his arms on the steering wheel and stares out the rain-spattered windscreen. "You can trust me," he says eventually, turning his head to face me. He pauses and a small half-smile appears. "I know that's what dodgy used car salesmen say, but you really can. I'm not going to let anything else bad happen to you."

It's hard to breathe all of a sudden, and a lump finds its way up my throat. "Thanks," I whisper. He doesn't have the power to promise that I won't get hurt, but I appreciate the sentiment. He's all I've got and I need to trust him.

An hour later we stop and dump the stolen car, switching it out for a small red rental car that shudders whenever it goes too fast. Even though I try to convince him not to, Seth buys another cell phone.

"We'll need it to contact your father when we get to New York," he says.

I can't think of an argument against that—other than the paranoia against them that Jeff instilled in me—so I just watch as he buys the cheapest one he can find.

By the time we get to our next motel in Eddyville, a tiny town about five hours' drive south of Quincy and hidden in the middle of the Shawnee National Forest, I've told Seth everything that happened in Quincy as well. We're sitting on the bed in the tiny room, eating chips and chocolate bars from the vending machine.

"I think there's a chance you might actually be a dragon, Mei."

A chip goes down the wrong way, and I can't breathe. I cough up the sharp pieces of potato and try not to choke, while Seth thumps me on the back.

My eyes are watering, and I don't know if I'm crying or if it's a reaction to choking. I wipe the moisture away and lean back against the rickety headboard, my shoulder touching Seth's.

"I know," I whisper. I let the shivers take me for a second, their uncontrollable nature helping push aside the fear that's hovering over me.

"It's not such a bad thing, you know."

"It seems like a terrible thing." I look up into his eyes. "They'll hunt me for the rest of my life. I'll never have any peace."

Seth shakes his head. "You can go away, find somewhere safe. They can't look everywhere."

I sniff sadly. I've already lived that life. "There are always people willing to give you up. Whether it's for the money, or because they're afraid, or even just angry about some perceived wrong."

He's silent for a moment. "Your father will know what we should do."

I move my legs restlessly. The closer we get to New York, the more I begin to doubt my father. I try to imagine him helping us for anything other than his own benefit and I struggle. He's never shown an interest in me before.

Whether it's because I'm a decoy dragon and not really his child, or if he's just not concerned with his own daughter—either way it doesn't show him in a good light. "I don't know..."

"What can we do, except stick to our original plan? Find your father, get him to tell us the whole story. Then you can decide what to do from there."

"Amos knows where we're going." I remind him. "They'll be chasing us every step of the way. And officially, the SIG and the Earthbound have an agreement. They're working together, on the same side."

"We'll be careful. And we'll find a way to meet with your father that they won't expect."

"I guess." I pause, thoughts smashing around inside my head. Who to trust, what to do. I wasn't sure about any of it. I put my hand to the little blue bottle that I've tied to string and hung around my neck. It feels warm against my collarbone. I don't know what the hell I'm going to do with my demon either, but I'm not going to let him out of my sight until I can figure it out. Yet another problem to sort out.

"Before we decide, I think we should open the box," says Seth.

We both look to where it's sitting in the corner of the room, next to the television. After the experience at the pawn shop, I couldn't bring myself to open it in the car.

It seems like the ideal thing to do right now, though.

Seth stands up and grabs the box, handing it to me where I sit on the bed. I sit up straighter, leaning over the box, tracing my finger over the intricate patterns. "Do they mean anything to you? The patterns?"

Seth shakes his head. "No. They seem... familiar. But I don't know what they mean."

I turn the box so the lid and its lock are facing me. The lock is built into the box, a circle that can be moved around with a strange mix of numbers and letters. I turn it gingerly, and every time it turns to a new digit, it clicks loudly.

"Do you know the code?" Seth leans in.

I shake my head. Jeff wouldn't do something as simple as leave me the damn code. It's going to require some quick thinking on my part to unlock the box. Smashing it open is also a bad idea; I'm pretty sure Jeff would have booby-trapped it.

Narrowing my eyes, I look at the numbers and letters. A date? A birthday? No, too obvious.

What about an address? I try the address of Si's hideaway, but only get five digits in before the box starts to hum angrily at me. "Guess not," I mutter to myself.

"What about your birthday?" Seth suggests.

I glare at him out of the corner of my eye, but put the date in anyway, just to prove I know what I'm doing. The box is humming like an angry buzzy bee who's just seen someone cutting down all his trees. "Nope," I say.

Coordinates to somewhere? I try to think of some of the places we've been more than once. Jeff always made me memorize the coordinates of places, and this seems like a good reason for that.

I try a couple of the ones I know off the top of my head. I even try a couple of obscure ones. The box just jumps a little at us and continues to hum angrily.

"Is there a time limit on this, do you think?" Seth asks nervously. "A self-destruct sequence if you put too many numbers in?"

I shrug, unable to deny that it would fit with Jeff to have something like that in the locking mechanism. "If there is, we need to hurry." I pause, tapping one finger against my lips. "What do you know about the dragons? Was there somewhere they used to live or hangout more than others?"

Seth shrugs. "Maybe their hatching grounds? Or where the young dragons used to live."

A little blip of excitement knocks about in my chest. "Where would that be?"

Seth picks up his cell phone and starts to search. I wait impatiently, trying not to fidget while he frowns at his screen. As I watch him, I realize he's logging into his cloud storage portal at the SIG. "Seth, your phone. They can find us through your phone if you log on."

He glances up at me and shakes his head. "Not the Earthbound. The SIG phone networks are secured against outside infringement."

"But the SIG can find us."

He shrugs. "Sure. But would that be so bad? We're heading in that direction anyway."

I open my mouth to disagree, but find I can't. Jeff and Si taught me to take care of myself and stay off the grid. But there's such a thing as being too paranoid. The SIG aren't the enemy.

"Here it is! I knew I'd filed it. An old historic site in Russia. Home of the main dragon hatching grounds. Not very well preserved these days, but here are the coordinates. Give it a go."

I slowly press the coordinates into the front of the box. The angry buzzing starts to diminish straight away, and by the time I've entered the last number and pressed the enter key, I know it's the right code. The box is humming gently in a satisfied tone that sends feelings of peace and calm through my body.

Turning the lock in the middle, I hear it click, and the lid slowly opens.

Holding my breath, I peer inside. All I can see at first are papers, lots of them. Documents, photos, and even a small book. I frown, wondering how Jeff thought all this would help me. "What were you doing, Jeff?" I mutter.

I pull out a photo, and it's of a small mountain somewhere lush with green grass and rolling pastures. I frown and turn it over.

The date is written on the back: *23 August, 1954. Ireland. Dragon site 3.*

"Dragon site 3?" I say.

"Some kind of old burial sites?" Seth suggests, leaning over my shoulder to look closer at the photo.

"Who knows." I shrug, picking up a document.

"The Supernatural Intelligence Group Dragon Subgroup," I read out. "Formed to confirm the existence of dragons in the current century." I scroll down the list of names in the group and find not only my father's name, but Jeff's as well.

It's dated two years before I was born.

27

Dragons are believed to have survived into the current era by lying dormant in various locations around the world.

The notes on the documentation are at various times confusing, terrifying, and vague. "So, the SIG has been researching the possibility that dragons aren't actually extinct," I say slowly.

Seth lifts his shoulders. "Sounds like it. What made them set this up? Does it say?"

I rifle through the pages and come to an old newspaper article about earthquakes and a flood in China affecting thousands of people. One line is highlighted. *"Eye witnesses said the buckling of the earth was so great, it was like the earth was rising up to the sky."*

"It seems a sketchy reason to start investigating the existence of dragons," I say.

"Maybe someone from the agency saw something. And this is just an extension of that."

I finger the pages, trying to get a bearing. "You know what this means, right?"

"That Jeff knew about you?"

I nod. "If I'm a dragon, Jeff knew about it. And he didn't tell me." I'd always suspected it, but this is confirmation. I try not to feel hurt, but it's hard. He kept me deliberately in the dark for all this time. And to what purpose? My life isn't better because I didn't know who and what I was earlier. If anything, the opposite is true.

I pick up the slim book that has shifted to the bottom of the box. It's from the supernatural publishing realms. *"An Historical Glimpse at Dragons: Their Lives Through Anthropological Discovery and Eye Witness Accounts."*

"Eye witness accounts?" I mutter. "Who the hell was alive three hundred years ago?"

Seth watches me carefully. "Some of the older races. The mountains probably have old ones who have lived that long."

I blink. Of course they do. On average, supernaturals live longer than humans. Two hundred years is a common average. So three hundred years isn't such a stretch for some of them. It probably seems like yesterday.

I flick through the pages, stopping on one that talks about how dragons shift. "This doesn't even make sense. They're not telling me how to do it; they're just describing what one person thought they saw."

"Well, I'm sure they weren't expecting the book to be a guide for a dragon who didn't know how to be a dragon," Seth says softly. I look up quickly, startled by his words.

He's right though. I *am* looking through the pages hoping it will tell me what to do. And maybe give me a few pointers on what being a dragon might mean for me.

"Does it say what happens to a dragon when they turn twenty?" Seth asks.

Turning twenty and coming into your full supernatural

powers can be mystical, or it can be painful, depending on the species. I thought I knew what to expect, but now I'm not so sure.

I shake my head. "I can't see anything yet, anyway." I'm thumbing through the pages when I come across a heading. *"A baby dragon nest."*

The picture on the page shows a large nest made of sticks. Inside the nest are small baby dragons, blowing out smoke and flames. "If I'm a dragon, how come I've never been in the shape of a dragon?" I ask. "Shouldn't I have shifted before now?" I'm relieved to have proof that I can't be a dragon after all.

I glance behind me to where Seth is leaning back. He's close over my shoulder, and turning has meant our faces are close. I feel the heat of his body warming mine. I swallow and move back slightly.

His eyes flash golden, like they do when he's struggling with a strong emotion, and then his face is neutral again. "There's a chance you're not. Maybe there's another reason you can call lightning to your hands. Maybe there are other creatures that can roar and push back a demon."

I stare at him a moment. "Are you trying to be funny?"

He doesn't move. "No."

I scowl. "Name something."

"Water demons." His face is so close to mine, I can see the tiny individual flecks of burnished gold in his hazel eyes.

"Oh, that's so much better. I'm a demon." I look away, trying to cover up the blush that's warming my cheeks.

"I'm sure there are old unnamed earth elementals who can do what you've done."

"Do you really think so?" I'm not sure whether to be glad.

One tiny—and stupid—part of me is secretly delighted

by the thought of being the only dragon in the world. The majority of me knows and understands how bad it would be. If I'm a dragon, it will make my life hell. Forever. But that tiny part of me can't help wondering what it would be like to be a dragon. To be that special.

"Do you think I'm a dragon, Seth? Be honest."

His face goes tight for a moment, and I can see he's struggling with his answer.

He shakes his head. "I don't know. Everything is pointing in that direction. The Earthbound think you are. But I can't reconcile what I know about you with the stories of the Dragon Wars. They were so brutal. The dragons didn't care about the death and destruction they caused for humans and supernaturals." He stares into my eyes, and I start tingling all over.

"You're not like that, Mei. You think of other people. You care." He reaches up and puts a hand against my face, rubbing his thumb along my cheek. He leans in and brushes his lips softly against mine, and it's as if the air around me has suddenly disappeared.

I can't breathe; I can't think.

28

Seth pulls back sharply and stands up. "I'm sorry. I shouldn't have done that." He wipes a hand across his mouth as if he's trying to destroy the evidence.

"Why not?" I say. Was it that bad for him? My lips are still buzzing with sensation.

"I'm an SIG Agent. It's my duty to protect you. I shouldn't be..." He waves his hand at me to indicate the kiss.

"I don't see why not." I fold my arms over my chest.

"There's every reason why not. That can never happen again," he says severely.

"It was just a kiss, no big deal." He's making me angry, which in turn is making me lash out.

It was more than just a kiss for me. I felt it right into my darkest core.

"That's right. It was just a meaningless kiss," he snaps. "I'm bored and lonely, and you're the nearest female." He sneers at me, but it doesn't reach his eyes. "It can't happen again." Seth strides over to the bathroom and locks the door behind him.

I stare at the closed door for a while, biting my lip softly.

When the shower starts up, I sigh and look back down at the box. It was nice, kissing Seth. Better than nice.

Traveling around all the time means I haven't had much experience with guys. It's almost a cliché that I should get a crush on the first handsome young SIG Agent who happens to land on my doorstep. I refuse to let him get under my skin.

I have more important things to worry about—like how I'm going to survive.

Something glitters at the bottom of the box, and I reach for it, pushing back the mismatched piles of documents and other paraphernalia that Jeff obviously thought would be useful. It's a delicate gold ring with a small diamond setting glittering under the light from the dusty light bulb over my head. When I look at it through the spell web, it doesn't even register as a blip.

I tip my head to one side, but I can't resist; I try the ring on.

It fits so snugly around my finger, it's like it's made for me. I'm still admiring it, holding my hand out at arm's length, when Seth opens the door to the bathroom. He's wearing the same clothes, but his hair is wet; it's the only clue he's taken a shower.

I put my hand down in my lap and look up at him expectantly.

He pulls the blanket from the bottom of the bed, and lays it folded up on the carpet. "I'll sleep on the floor tonight," he says, before lying down and facing away from me.

A few minutes ago, I might have been distraught at this treatment, but I'm distracted now by the ring. I feel it thrumming along my veins. I can't believe it's not showing up on the spell web. It feels more powerful than anything in the old man's pawnshop cellar.

I've been staring at the ring on my finger for a while when I glance up at the clock on the bedside table. It's midnight, Seth is snoring next to me, and it's dark.

All of a sudden, the urge to be outside takes over. I have to get out of our tiny room and get into nature. To experience it, to breathe it in. Eddyville is a tiny dot of a town in the middle of the Shawnee National Forest.

It's a freaking nature reserve. I'm going to explore it.

The car keys are on the table, and I grab them on my way past. I hesitate at the table next to the branded notepad, but reason wins out. I scrawl a note saying I'm going to visit nature.

As soon as I'm in the car and driving down the small backroad, surrounded on both sides by trees and nature, I let out a howl. I glance at the ring on my finger, sparkling in the moonlight. I feel bright and alive for the first time in years. Maybe ever.

Up ahead is a sign for a waterfall, and suddenly I'm eager to feel water on my body, just like at Si's house. It's only been days, but it feels like years since I was there, hiding away from the world with my two mentors. I didn't have a care in the world back then, in the good old days.

I push my foot down on the accelerator, and I whip up the narrow, windy roads until I reach the parking lot at the end of the road. I have to walk from here. Pounding along the nature track, I keep my hand out in front of me so I can see the ring. It's so beautiful.

My foot snags on something and I tumble forward, landing heavily on the forest floor. My heart beating fast, I look back and swear at the tree root clearly sticking up.

I need to pay attention.

I've left Seth sleeping back at the motel, and who knows when he'll wake up and see my note. I've also got the car, our only form of transport. If I break my ankle out here, there's no one to save me. The darkness pushes down on me for a moment, the night sounds become menacing.

But then I hold up my hand, and the diamond twinkles merrily in the moonlight. I smile. Nothing will go wrong. I'll go for a decadent midnight swim at a waterfall, let myself feel at one with nature, and be back at the motel for breakfast, before Seth even knows I've gone.

The path leads up over rocks and tree roots, with the occasional set of stairs to help. Trees curl over me, and I feel like they're protecting me from the world, holding me tight against their bodies. I feel safe for the first time in days.

I hear the waterfall before I see it. The energy created by water pounding against rocks is unmistakable and I quicken my steps. I burst out into a clearing, and there it is before me.

My power and magic are rising inside me. Before I can think about what I'm doing, I start pulling off my clothes, leaving my shorts, t-shirt, underwear and sandals scattered on the grassy verge near the water.

Without even a glance into the depths, I dive naked into the pool. A thought whispers past my brain that it's dangerous to dive into a pool I've never been in before. But I'm already in the water, and it's fine. The moon above provides light, and the water surrounding me feels like home.

It's as if the last couple of days have been a dream.

I swim slowly around the pool, and then lie under the waterfall, letting the water beat down on my naked skin. It's therapeutic and restorative, and by the time I've had enough, I feel like I could take on the world.

A flicker of gold on my finger catches the moonlight.

It's telling me to do something, but it's not clear, the images are vague.

All of a sudden, I'm tired.

There's a patch of ground nearby, covered in moss and leaves. Without thinking, I swim over and pull myself out of the pool. Stretching my arms high, I yawn, then curl up onto my side and go to sleep.

29

Water is coming, curling and streaming down the small valley, swiping at everything in its path, creating destruction and chaos. It is the king, the one all others must bow to.

It can pull down mighty trees, crush rocks, and destroy the buildings created by the puny humans. It is the master of life. None may survive the wrath of water.

And water is the toy of the dragon. The dragon rules water, as water rules every other element.

I blink awake, rub my eyes, and look around. It's early morning; there's a layer of dew on the undergrowth and the birds are singing their wake-up songs. The water beside me is agitated and rough, the waterfall raging slightly higher than I remember from last night.

I glance down at my body and blush. I'm still naked. I have been all night, since I curled up in this spot. It's not like me; I don't usually sleep buck naked in the middle of an unfamiliar forest. It's not that I'm shy, it's just not the safest thing in the world to do. My clothes are where I dropped them, a few feet away, and I pull my them on, staring up at the waterfall as I do it.

There's something wrong. I can feel it. The water is running faster and stronger than it should be. There's something pushing at it, hurrying it along, like a little whippet at its feet.

I recall dreams of water, with pounding waves that crush everything in their path. Glancing nervously upstream, I know I have to find out what the problem is; I have a horrible suspicion it's something to do with me.

I don't have walking shoes on; my current sandals are more for beach wear. But I have no choice. I start up the path at the side of the waterfall, treading carefully on the steep steps. I get to the top and the valley falls away below me, the trees hugging tightly to the water, creating a beautiful hidden wilderness.

Further down the valley, I can see a small clearing with a couple of pup tents. It must be the local camping ground.

Upstream, it's not quite as peaceful. A rumbling noise is obvious up here, and in the distance, I see a huge wave of water pushing its way along the path of the river. It's massive, not a wave that should be possible given the size of the river.

But I can see it.

And I think I created it in my dreams.

I turn back downriver toward the camp ground. I have to warn them, or they're going to drown before they even wake up. The water is moving so fast, I don't know how I'm going to get there in time. But I have to try.

I climb down the side of the waterfall and start running along the edge of the river.

"Mei!" It's Seth. He's standing at the edge of the clearing, anger thundering across his features.

"No time to yell at me," I say as I run past. "We have to warn the campers."

I glance behind me, and he's still standing, unmoving.

"Hurry! There's a huge wave coming. They'll drown if we don't get them out of here."

He sighs, and then starts running, easily catching up to me in the undergrowth. "Don't think this means we won't have a conversation about what you're doing out here."

"How did you find me?"

"Intuition."

"You've got another bug on me?" It's the only explanation. I know I didn't give that much information away in my note.

"Turns out my instinct to put a bug on your clothes was right, wasn't it?"

I open my mouth to argue, but it doesn't matter. Not at the moment. I have to make it to the campsite before that wave does.

Several minutes later, I'm puffing like we've run a marathon, and it doesn't feel like we're any closer to the campsite. "We're not going to make it," I say.

"How far is the campsite?"

"Maybe another half mile along the river. But look at it," I say, gesturing to the roiling, tumbling water next to us. It looks like it's just seen a month of torrential rain and is struggling to escape the banks of the river.

"What if we jump in the river and flow down with it?" Seth suggests.

I look at him and then at the river. It's a dangerous notion; I can tell the river isn't going to be easy. But what choice do we have? "Okay, let's do it."

"We'll have to remove some clothes. We'll get water-logged and sink to the bottom otherwise."

I give him a look, but he's right. I pull off my T-shirt and jeans shorts, and I'm standing there in my bra and undies. "Come on, we have to hurry." I walk into the water and start swimming downstream without checking to see if Seth is following me.

He's right, this way is faster, but it's also scarier.

Rocks pop up from under the water, and I've bashed myself against at least two before I learn to stay in the middle and try to flow with the current. I'm pushing my arms through the water as well, trying to make myself move faster.

It'll be my fault if something happens to the people at the campground.

I glance behind me and my heart starts racing. There's a raging white water wave, not more than five hundred yards behind us.

"Hurry, Seth!" I turn back, and this time I'm using my magic to get me through the water. I've never done it before, but something inside me knows how, and soon I'm making double the time as the current picks me up and carries me downriver.

The tents are in sight when I feel a momentary switch in the direction of the water and air behind me. I turn, and there's the wave, now twenty yards behind me, gathering all the water around toward it. Seth is almost inside the wave, his body like a toy being tossed in the enormous wall of water.

My fists clench and I put my feet down on the floor of the river. He's not going to die here.

Not another person protecting me.

Just as Seth is about to be devoured by the wave, I manage to grasp the energy created by the wave and fling his body to the river bank. He scrambles to his feet and runs toward the three small tents that are about to be torn apart by the waves.

I turn back to the giant wave, watching as it tears trees from the ground, moving boulders like they're pebbles, and I open my arms, lifting them high.

I know water; it's my element. I might not be able to stop this giant monstrosity, but perhaps I can push it away from the people. The water all around me reacts instantly to my magic, but the wave is too strong, too much a force of its own. It keeps pounding toward me, and toward the tents. Out of the corner of my eye, I see Seth herding the campers out of their tents and as far back into the forest as he can get them.

And then it hits. It's like a concrete wall has fallen on me. I try to concentrate on forcing its path to the other side of the river, away from the people, but some part of me knows I have to focus on keeping myself alive. I can't breathe under water, and I'm currently being pushed under a wave the size of a house. I'm being toppled and turned, my body like a tiny stuffed doll in the raging waters. Something heavy hits my head, and the water turns red.

The world feels still and calm, despite the raging river, and when I see stars, I'm not surprised.

30

My head is pounding like there's a jackhammer beating at me, but I still don't open my eyes. I don't want to see whatever is out there, because I'm pretty convinced it's going to be bad.

I just lie—wherever I am—and soak up the fact that I'm still alive. Barely.

Eventually I give in. There's only so long that you can deny yourself the knowledge.

Squeezing open my eyes just a tiny bit, I can't see anything for the ridiculously bright light. I groan and close my eyes again, holding an arm up over my face.

"Mei? Are you awake?" Seth's voice comes from close by.

I nod slowly, but that just makes the jackhammers start up even harder. "How... How are the people?"

"They're fine. I got everyone out of the way of the wave. I... I came back for you, and found you beside the river."

I open my eyes a crack again. There's a subtext in his voice that I don't get. "What's wrong?" I ask, steeling myself for bad news.

His blurry face comes into view in front of me. I'm still

lying down, and I think it might be grass under my back. I'm not entirely sure, but it's soft, whatever it is.

"You... you weren't breathing. For a long time. I thought you were dead."

My eyes jack open fully, and I try to sit up. "What are you talking about?"

"You were just lying there. Not breathing. I... I called it in."

"Who to?" My head is pounding worse now. I don't know what's happening, but I know Seth's gone and told someone where we are.

"My supervisor."

"The one who probably informed to the Earthbound?"

Seth stands up, pacing agitatedly. "You were dead. It didn't matter anymore. And I don't have the phone number for anyone else. I told him to tell your father."

I try to feel horrified at the news my father is being told of my death, maybe even as I lie here taking it in. But a part of me thinks he deserves it after years of neglect.

Bet he regrets not spending more time with me now. "What did they say for you to do?"

"Wait here. That they'd be on their way soon."

"How long since you rang?"

"About half an hour."

I look around. "We need to get out of here. Right now." I look down. I'm wearing only my bra and undies.

Seth nods and helps me up. "I truly thought you were dead, Mei. I still... I don't understand how you're not dead." He pulls me into a tight hug that makes my eyes water.

I can feel his heart beating against my ear, and I close my eyes. The jackhammers subside slightly. "I know. Maybe it can even work to our advantage if they think I'm dead?"

"Maybe. But you're right. We need to get out of here

before the wrong people find us." He bends down and hands me a bundle; it's my clothes. I don't know how he found them, but I'm glad he did. I put them on quickly, and then Seth grabs my hand and pulls me along a trail.

My legs are wobbly at first, and I trip a couple of times. Luckily, Seth keeps me on my feet, and we keep moving forward. We emerge into the clearing where the tents were.

I gape as I take in the devastation of the campground. Nothing is the same as it was before, trees are uprooted, the ground has shifted, the edge of the river looks like it was ravaged by an enormous beast—which I guess it was.

"Is it like this the whole way up the river?" I whisper.

"In this section at least. That wave came out of nowhere and just took everything with it. Luckily, it's a pretty isolated section of the reserve, there weren't many people around. It goes for about another mile down river, and then it just seemed to lose momentum and die away. I've never seen anything like it."

My breathing is sketchy as I try to remember what happened. I was having crazy dreams about water and huge waves. Then I wake up and there's a massive wave heading my way. Not long after that I lose consciousness and the wave dies off.

I look down at my hand, to the ring.

It's gone. One part of me screams in frustration, because it had looked lovely on my finger and it had felt so right. But most of me knows the ring is to blame for my actions last night. The way it made me feel is like a lingering taste in my mouth, of honey and some kind of delicious spice. Under its influence, I ran off into the wilderness by myself, and swam naked under the stars. Nothing so very terrible in that—it's the giant tsunami that swept through the reserve I'm worried about. If anyone had been hurt here today it would have been my fault.

"Is this what you're looking for?" Seth asks softly. He holds up the ring. It sparkles in the early morning light.

Without thinking I reach out to grab it. Seth pulls his hand back out of reach and I force my arm back down.

"Keep it. It's not safe," I mutter. I want it back so badly, I know it can't be good for me. Or for anyone else.

"What happened, Mei?"

"Come on," I grind out between clenched teeth. I can't handle any more guilt. I'm weighed down as it is. "Let's get out of here."

We find the car and get going. We're driving down the long freeway on the north side of the National Forest when we see a row of black SUVs with tinted black windows speeding in the other direction.

"Not a moment too soon," I murmur.

"They'll figure out you're not dead."

"How?"

"No body. And why would I run?"

"You freaked out and decided to take my body for a decent burial." The lies come so easily to me. It's a lifetime of living under a pseudonym. "You need to ring your supervisor and let him know that's why you're not there. And then we're going to ditch that new phone of yours. If they didn't find us when you linked to your cloud account, they'll have traced you when you called in."

Seth nods absently, and I wonder if he disagrees. But at the next service station, he pulls in, makes a call on his phone, and then throws it into the dumpster out the back.

I watch him do all of this under hooded eyes. "Why are you still helping me?" I ask as we drive along the freeway.

Seth has always been there for me, but I can't get the image of Amos pointing a gun at me out of my head.

He glances my way, his fiery hazel eyes boring into mine. "I'm doing my duty. I was assigned to keep you safe and that's what I'm going to do." His words are bland, but there's something about the timbre of his voice that sends a tiny shiver along my skin.

"I don't think your supervisors actually want you to do that anymore," I say, crossing my arms over my chest to try and quell the ache inside me. He confuses me like no one else ever has.

"Doesn't matter. That's what they assigned me." He's watching the road now, and I see his knuckles whiten on the steering wheel.

Reluctant warmth spreads through my belly. Whatever his reason for being here with me, I'm glad he is.

I could probably do this alone if I had to, I know I could. But having Seth by my side makes it so much less lonely.

I just have to figure out the right time to come back from the dead and demand that my father tell me the truth.

I don't know whether to cry or to laugh. The laughing will be hysterical, and the crying might scare Seth. So I just smile tightly and turn to stare out the window.

We're okay for now.

31

We're almost to the outskirts of New York when I think to ask. "What did your supervisor say to you when you told him you'd run with the body?"

Seth grins. "He told me to get my butt back to the National Park. He was yelling."

"Did you say you weren't going to?" I watch Seth's amusement with fascination. This is a side of him I haven't seen. He's usually such a stickler for the rules.

"Nah. Let them think I'm contrite and heading back to them. It gives us more time." He's tapping one finger on the steering wheel in time to the music that's playing on the radio.

"What are we actually going to do, Seth?" I've had time to consider our situation, and I don't think we're doing the right thing any more. It feels like we're landing ourselves in the middle of a hornet's nest.

"We have to believe that your father doesn't want to hurt you. It's the only thing we can be sure of in this."

I nod, although I'm not positive on that point. "So we're still going to try and get to my dad?"

"Sure."

"They'll be on high alert."

"I was thinking about that. The Earthbound know where we're going, but would they tell the SIG? I'm not so sure.

"They'd want an edge over them, so they can get you back. We might be able to use that to our advantage. At the moment, as far as the majority of the SIG knows, I was guarding a minor asset who happened to die on my watch. Not a great look, but certainly nothing major."

"My father knows the full story, doesn't he?"

"But he's not in on every single decision, is he? He stays away from the higher-ups. He's the best agent we've got, but he's not renowned for playing well with others."

"So you think the SIG doesn't know I might be a dragon?" It's the first time I've said the words aloud and believed them. I feel the fluttering of something inside my belly, like a new awareness has taken over my body and it's assimilating to it.

He nods. "That's right. I think your father has kept it hidden all these years. So well hidden, it almost got you killed."

"If that's true, then how do we get into SIG headquarters and see my father?"

"We need to lure him out. Send him a coded message that only he will understand. If nothing else, Vincent will have SIG headquarters under surveillance. We're not going to get in easily."

"And for the coded message, you want me to think of something only my dad would know about me?" I bite my lip and stare out the windscreen.

Seth glances my way. "Would that be possible? Does he know you that well?"

It stings to hear him say it, but he's right. I can't think of anything that will alert my father and not everyone else. Jeff was more my father than Agent Damien Walker. I shake my head, keeping my gaze fixed out the window.

Seth clears his throat awkwardly. "I had this encounter with him at the academy. Just before I was assigned to you. He asked me a couple of questions about the... trouble I got into there."

"What happened?"

Scenery whips past the window. Seth is silent for such a long time, I think he's not going to answer. I can't imagine what he could have done that was so bad.

"There was someone being bullied," he says softly. "I didn't like it, so I took measures to ensure it didn't happen again."

"What kind of measures?"

"I'm pretty good with computers... I hacked into his bank accounts and took all his money, gave it away to charity. I did a few things to his SIG records, so he looked like he had a couple of black marks against him. Messed with his driver's license, gave him a few parking tickets. That kind of thing."

My eyes widened. "I wouldn't have picked you for a hacker."

"I'm not really. But I was just so mad."

"And what happened?"

"I made it clear that things like that would continue to happen if he kept bullying my friend."

"Did he stop?"

Seth sighed. "In a way. My friend left the SIG academy, said he wasn't cut out for it. The bully turned me in to the SIG watchdogs. Said I was the one bullying him."

"How did you not get thrown out too?"

"I don't know. At least, I didn't know for a long time. Now I think it might have been your father's influence. He's on the watchdog committee."

"So he vouched for you?"

"At the time, while I was in front of the tribunal, he was actually the harshest of them all. A real tough nut, wanted me to be thrown out. But a couple of days later, he was a different man. Kind of friendly. I was shocked, because he really had ripped me a new one in the tribunal hearing. Looking back, I realize he was playing a part."

"What makes you so sure?" I say, a little tartly. It's all supposition. And I can't help feeling a little jealous. He's damn well had more interaction with my father than I have.

It's not fair.

"He said something to me. It was really cryptic at the time, but now it makes more sense."

"What did he say?"

"Don't let her fly away, without knowing how to get to the nest."

I scrunch up my face. "And what the hell does that mean?"

"If you're a dragon, you're going to go through some kind of massive change when you turn twenty. And according to that book Jeff left us, the dragons usually did that at a nest of some kind."

"And how am I going to find this nest?" I say, sarcasm hard in my voice.

Seth shrugs. "I don't have that part figured out. That's why we're going to see your dad."

"And you think we should mention a nest to him?"

"It's just an idea. But it's a conversation that I think was about you, and only he and I will know about."

It's a good idea. I just wish there was some cute little conversation that I'd had with my father that we could use instead.

32

"Do you even know this kid?" I ask, crouching behind a bush in Central Park.

"Of course. He's run errands for me before."

"Do you trust him?"

"Not particularly. That's why I made sure to tip him really well and promise him money when he gets back. Nothing like more money to motivate."

"It's been more than forty-five minutes since you sent the message."

"I know. Just calm down. Maybe he didn't find your father straight away."

"What if he's not there?"

"He's there. There's a big meeting of the cadet academy faculty."

"He's not faculty."

"He always goes, don't worry."

I shift my position, trying to ease the cramp in my legs. If I'm a sodding dragon, surely I shouldn't have to suffer things like cramp and pins and needles?

"There he is," whispers Seth triumphantly.

An older man is walking slowly down the exact path we told him to, his gaze fixed ahead of him, like he doesn't have a care in the world. He's wearing a suit, but it's a relaxed look, his tie loosened, his jacket undone. He's got a bit of silver in his hair, but he looks fit and healthy. One hand is in his trouser pocket, and he's wearing dark glasses against the glare of the sun.

"What do we do now?" I whisper back.

"I approach him with the news that you're not dead after all."

"I'm coming too." I make to stand, but Seth puts one hand on my arm. "I think you should stay here. Wait until I've confirmed it's okay."

"It's fine. He's my dad." I hesitate. "Probably."

Seth shakes his head. "You never know. He could have been compromised. When I put my hand in my left pocket, you know it's safe to come out. But not before then." He glares down at me, like he knows I'm planning to ignore his precautions. "Promise me, Mei. Just do it my way, this time?"

I shrug, but can't look away from the intensity in his eyes. "Okay, fine. I'll wait for your signal."

He smiles and puts one hand briefly on my shoulder.

Then he's gone, heading off at a crouching run to the other side of the wooded copse we've been hiding in for the last forty-five minutes.

I watch as Seth approaches my father. I find it hard to attach any significance to this man in front of me, SIG agent Damien Walker. He's covered in the spell web, but it's muted, like he's got something covering it. Vincent said he was hiding the fact that he was supernatural, so I guess that's why. I narrow my eyes, trying to see him better. There should be some kind of connection, shouldn't there? Maybe a recognition deep in my gut that he was part of my creation?

But there's nothing. He could be anyone. Just some old guy walking in the park at lunchtime.

Agent Walker stares at Seth as he approaches. He shakes his hand, placing his other hand on Seth's shoulder.

They continue walking along the path and Seth talks to him for a few minutes. My father listens intently, before putting one hand out to stop Seth in his tracks. He asks Seth something, and Seth shakes his head. I try to read their lips, to figure out what's happening.

I'm concentrating so hard on what's happening out on the path in front of me, I don't notice anything else until rough hands grab me from behind, lock my arms, and place handcuffs around my wrists. I twist and turn, but whoever is behind me is strong.

"Eagle One, we have her. I repeat. We have the target." The low voice is speaking into a headset.

I turn and see my father and Seth surrounded by SIG agents as well. My first thought is that he's been followed, and I feel immediate regret that I've brought him into my mess. But then I see him step away from Seth, who is handcuffed and held by four brawny agents.

He's part of it.

33

Before I can make another move, or at least try, a black canvas bag is shoved over my head, and my legs are tied together tight with zip wire. Handcuffs are fastened just a little too tight over my wrists. I'm hefted over my attacker's shoulder. How the hell is he going to carry a body out of Central Park without anyone noticing?

Then I'm dumped into the back of some kind of trash can, my head hitting the side painfully, and it all becomes clear.

It smells bad, and there's something soft and mushy under my thigh that I'm trying not to think about. It's a relief when I'm transferred into the back of a vehicle, although this is short-lived, because now I'm worried about where they're taking me.

Us.

They took Seth as well, even though he's an agent.

I'm hoping they'll take us back to SIG headquarters. At least there's some sense of official procedure with SIG. It might be a covert agency, but surely they wouldn't let an innocent person be murdered?

It's all I have to hold on to.

I'm alone in the back of the car when it moves off. I can't see anything or move more than a couple of inches. I don't bother sitting up, and when the car goes on an angle into what feels like an underground garage, my breathing gets messed up, and I focus on not hyperventilating inside the black material sack.

The car stops and the same rough hands drag me out of the backseat, holding my arm tight. Someone cuts the ties at my legs, and I hear other doors slamming around me. "Seth?" I say.

"I'm here, Mei." Seth grunts as if someone has hit him, and I keep quiet. I reach out along the spell web. At least if I can find Seth's patchy section of the grid, I'll be able to breathe easier. But there's nothing there. Literally nothing. It's like the extreme silence of noise-cancelling headphones, when you're used to having people yelling all around you.

I try not to give in to the panic that's crawling inside me, but I feel like I'm going to collapse in on myself without the support of the spell web.

Luckily for me, the hands on my arm don't let go, and when the rest of the group moves, they pull me forward. I hear the ding of an elevator, and then I'm led into the confined space. I feel bodies close to mine, the heat reaching out to me. I shiver, despite the warmth.

It seems like forever before the elevator stops and the doors open.

"Where are you taking me?" I ask as we walk along a hallway. The only way I can tell is from the way our footsteps seem to echo around us.

No one answers, but I hear the breathing of several other people. I try to isolate the sounds, to confirm numbers. Si would be proud. There's a heavy breather, someone with either a large nose, or maybe a broken nose. Then a shifty breather who isn't breathing regularly, and a sniffer who's driving me bonkers with his runny nose. There are more, but I'm proud of myself for managing to isolate even those three.

Plus, it's distracted me for a few minutes.

We continue down the hallway. A door opens and I'm shoved inside. No one follows me and the door closes.

I stand uncertainly for a moment trying to get my bearings. Nothing moves, and I seem to be alone in the room. Quickly lying down on my back, I pull my handcuffed hands down past my butt and bent legs, until my cuffed hands are in front of me.

Another trick of Si's.

Then I stand up again, and lift my handcuffed hands to my head. The canvas bag is tied on with rope, and I awkwardly start to pull it undone.

My fingers are clumsy, and I can't make them work properly inside the too-tight cuffs. It takes me forever, but eventually I drag off the head covering and suck in fresh air.

Once I can breathe normally again, I look around.

The room itself is strange. It has some form of metal cladding on all the walls, floor and ceiling. There's no handle on this side of the door, and there are no windows, just a chair and a bed to one side. I frown when I realize they mean for me to stay here long enough to need a bed.

The next thing I notice is the camera in the top corner recording everything I'm doing.

I touch the metal wall, the black handcuffs cold against my skin. I'm expecting the wall to be equally cold, but it's warm and lets off a faint buzzing vibration. It seeps into my hands and I pull away. I can't sense anything outside this room, not even my strongest element, water.

I pace the room, six steps by six steps, trying to figure out a way to escape, but there are no bolts to loosen, no vents to undo, not even a gust of air to indicate they're giving me enough oxygen to breathe. Even if I could find a way out, my hands are still tied together, making everything way more difficult.

Visions of Vincent's men throwing me into the water tank and the furnace make my legs wobble and I sit down onto the bed.

Are they going to start testing me here, too? I don't know if I'm a dragon or not, but perhaps there's more of a chance I'd survive whatever they throw at me?

But perhaps I wouldn't. I still don't feel like a dragon. I definitely don't look like one.

There's nothing else to do but wait. Someone will have to come and get me eventually.

I've been avoiding thinking about him, but now I can't help it. My father did this. He helped the SIG capture me and lock me up here.

What does it mean? Is he doing it because he thinks it's in my best interests? Or because he's not really my father?

I lie back on the bed, my hands clasped on my stomach, looking up at the metal ceiling. My thoughts run across my consciousness, and I try to sort through them.

Who can I trust? Why would they lock me up here? What have they done with Seth? Am I really a dragon?

I don't know the answers, and it's driving me nuts. I clench my fists into tight balls, and let out a growl of frustration.

Then I sigh. As Jeff would've said, that kind of useless emotion won't get me anywhere.

My gaze locks on the camera in the corner and its red blinking light. It occurs to me that I might be able to get them to come to me sooner rather than later. Waiting just seems like a waste of everyone's time.

Walking over to the camera, I jump up and manage to knock it a little with both hands. It moves back into position. I leap up again and hit it, this time with more force.

It moves back again.

The third time, I wrap my handcuffs around the back of the camera where it's attached to the wall, and I'm dangling there, pulling on it, when the door opens. This time I see my burly guard.

"Hey. Stop that," he says, his voice a surly growl.

He pulls on me, and the extra force rips the camera off its hinges. We both fall to the floor and end up lying in a heap on the metal ground, his arms still tight around my middle.

"The other girl didn't cause trouble," the guard mutters. "You're obviously the dumb one."

I elbow him in the ribs and stamp on his shins. If I'm the dumb one, I may as well be really stupid.

He grunts in pain, but before he can retaliate, another figure appears in the doorway. "MacKenzie, if you can't control one small woman, you'll be reassigned."

My father.

34

The guard lets go of my middle and I roll away. He drags himself to his feet and grudgingly reaches down with one arm and helps me to my feet as well. "She destroyed the camera, sir."

It's only as I'm standing next to him rubbing my now-grazed wrists that I realize what he said.

What other girl?

"I can see that, MacKenzie," my father is saying. "She's due in room seven for questioning now, anyway. Bring her." His face is bland, unconcerned, like it's nothing special that he's helped the SIG to lock me up and throw away the key.

The guard pulls me toward the door, his hands digging into my arms. My father is waiting outside the door, but I don't look at him again. This is all his fault.

I'm led to a room just down the hall. The door opens and another stranger in a suit stands there, looking at me expectantly. "I'll take her from here, MacKenzie. Wait outside," he says.

He stands back and waves me into the room. It has the same metal casing, but with a metal table and chairs in the middle. There's also a door at the other end of the room with an efficient-looking computerized lock on it.

My father enters the room after me and shuts the door with a small but particular click of the lock. "I'll take it from here, Agent Harkness."

"Yes, sir. I'll wait outside." The agent nods at my father and walks to the locked door. Instead of opening it, he simply slides through it. I gape at him. There's a metal worker in the SIG?

"Sit, please, Mei. You're making me nervous with all your standing."

I glare down at him and look pointedly at the handcuffs on my wrist. I'm not going to do anything he says until he stops treating me like a prisoner.

And if he was ever nervous, I'll eat my hat. If I had a hat.

"I'm not allowed to take those off. Not until I've secured your cooperation." He holds his hands out wide, as if there's nothing he can do.

"You're not going to secure anything from me if you don't take these damn handcuffs off," I say, glaring at him. After everything I've been through in the last few days, intimidation and lying from my father isn't going to throw me.

He sighs and stands up, pulling a set of keys out of his pocket. "I'm going to get in trouble for this," he says. There's a small knowing half-smile on his face, and I want to slap it away. Who the hell does he think he is?

The handcuffs come off, and I rub my wrists, working the circulation back in. "Now tell me why you double-crossed us."

"Sit, and I'll explain it all." He waves to the chair opposite. Then sighs when I remain standing. "There was no double-cross. Just a case of handling a couple of runaways who'd gotten themselves in over their heads."

He walks around behind me and puts one hand on my shoulder. He leans in. "If you want to live through this, sit down and shut the hell up," he mutters into my ear in a hard voice that's nothing like the charming tone he's been using.

I glance up at the camera above our heads, then sit.

My brain is whirring with possibilities. Perhaps this isn't as simple as I thought. When he sits across from me, the jovial expression is back in place. It's almost like I'm in a room with two people. The jovial man in front of me, and the hard-edged agent who told me to sit. I can't keep up.

"Where's Seth?"

"He's being debriefed. He *is* technically a rogue agent."

"It wasn't his fault. He was told to protect me; that was all he was trying to do."

"Despite orders to the contrary from his supervisor?"

"He had reason to believe his supervisor tipped off the Earthbound to our whereabouts."

"Tell me more about his accusations."

"Tell me what this is about," I counter. I'm not going to get Seth in trouble.

"All in good time. First I want you to tell me what happened after you left the hideout."

"You mean after we were attacked by the Earthbound and Jeff and Si were brutally murdered because of a mole in the SIG?" I ask.

"Yes. After that." His expression doesn't change. I'm beginning to see why my father is such a good agent. He's holding himself so tightly behind his mask, it's impossible to know what he's thinking or feeling underneath the charming exterior he presents to the world.

"We drove to a small town I know. Seth was shot, and I needed someone to heal him. Then we were captured by the Earthbound. They took us to their secret lair. Which by the way is not so secret now, because I can tell you exactly where it is."

"Please do. We're always keen for more information on our allies."

"Ah, yes, your allies. I forgot that you're on their side." I give him my best snide look.

It bounces off him without even leaving a dent. "We have a long-standing agreement with the Earthbound."

"Then why have they been trying to kill me since I was a child?"

"They haven't been very successful at it, you must admit."

I pause. "It actually turns out they only wanted to capture me for the last few years."

He raises his eyebrows and nods. "That fits, I suppose. What happened then?"

"They held us prisoner, and the Earthbound leader Vincent informed me I was a dragon." I watch my father's face closely. A tiny twitch appears at the corner of his eye, but nothing else. "I told him he was insane, that of course I wasn't a dragon. He then tried to kill me to prove his point."

I take a couple of breaths and glance around the metal room. It reminds me of the furnace, and I have to pull my hands off the table and clasp them together in my lap to keep my father from seeing how much they're trembling.

"But he obviously didn't succeed."

"No." I don't elaborate. "After almost dying at the hands of a lunatic, his son Amos to helped me escape. Seth, Amos, and I went on a small road trip. Then Amos had a change of heart and tried to return me to his father. Seth and I escaped again and here we are." I spread my arms wide to indicate my current position and glare at my father.

"How did you shoot down the helicopter?"

I shrug. "It was hit by lightning. They shouldn't have been out in a storm."

"What happened in the national park?" he asks.

I frown. "What do you mean?"

"The massive wave that destroyed the camping grounds."

I bite my lip. "I don't know. A freak of nature?" I have no logical explanation for that wave. But do I have to explain it? Just because I was there, doesn't mean it was my fault.

I finger the small blue bottle tied around my neck and consider telling him about the pawnshop and all the dangerous goodies out the back.

That I'm thinking I might actually be a dragon, after all.

But I can't. I won't. I'm still too mad at him to offer him anything.

"I know that's not what happened, Mei." He sounds tired. I always thought of him as this renegade agent, who travelled the world and could spin a situation on a dime. Turns out that was just a dream, an illusion I created to make myself feel better about him neglecting me.

"Then what's the truth? Tell me what this is all about." I lean forward across the table and place both my hands palm down on the metal surface. I stare directly into his eyes, pushing through his mask, to the real man behind. "*Tell me why I'm here.*"

35

His face pales, but that's the only indication that my words have affected him. I lean back in my chair with a huff of breath and wait. My gaze doesn't leave his face however, and he starts squirming. I don't know how I know, because his bland expression is still in place, but I do.

Will he tell me I'm a dragon? Or that I'm not a dragon? I don't even care which it is at this point. I just want to move on with my life in one direction or another.

He clears his throat and taps one finger against the table and then stops. The silence feels enormous, like it could never be filled even if one of us speaks.

But I wait. Jeff has been training me since I was eight years old. He was the master of the uncomfortable moment, the awkward silence. It's almost like breathing to me.

My father breaks first, although it's not so much breaking as giving in to the inevitable. "There are two of you. Two babies born on the same day. One of you is a dragon, and one of you is not."

"So the story Vincent told me is true? About a dragon child?"

He shakes his head. "I doubt it. The Earthbound have their own version of these stories, and they often don't match the truth." He pauses, staring at me through narrowed eyes, as if trying to see inside me. I hold my breath.

Eventually he speaks again. "I was in China on assignment for the SIG. We were trying to confirm rumors that the dragon race hadn't died out as we had previously believed. There had been sightings and it turned out it was true. An earthquake in the region had woken an ancient dragon from her hibernation. While I was in the region, I met and fell in love with a beautiful woman. I didn't know she was the dragon Xinglong, who I was there to find, until it was too late."

"So you turned on her and killed her?" I can't keep the bitterness from my voice.

"Of course not. I tried to protect her. I helped her hide in a village far from where she'd been sighted. We were married, and lived together while she was pregnant. Except just before our baby was due, I was called away urgently and wasn't with her when she went into labor. She gave birth without me there, with the help of a local nurse." He stops and swallows hard, clearly trying to mask strong emotions. "Just days after she gave birth, the Earthbound found and attacked our home. They destroyed it, killing almost everyone inside, including my beloved Xinglong." He pauses and I see a crack in his mask. He's telling the truth. "I didn't return in time to save her."

"I'm sorry," I say. I can see this story is still painful for him.

Taking a deep, raw breath, my father continues. "While I was searching the rubble, I heard the sound of crying. I found two tiny babies hidden inside a metal box deep in the basement. One belonged to Xinglong's wet nurse, and the other child was my daughter."

"Why did you take both babies?"

My father looks up at me with haunted eyes. "The wet nurse died with my wife. There was no one else to look after the second baby. But also, they were both so little. I couldn't tell..." He lets the sentence dangle and stares at me with a hopeless expression.

I feel my jaw drop. "You couldn't tell which was which?"

"The wet nurse had wrapped both of you in matching swaddles, and you were both so young. The same brown eyes, the same dark downy hair, and even the same rounded heads. I'd never met my own child. I couldn't tell which one was my own damn daughter." His voice is rough.

"So you brought both of us back to the US?"

He nods.

"Which one am I?" Surely they know now? Except... Why tell me this whole story if he knew?

He clears his throat. "We've never been able to tell. Tests were done when you were babies. We could tell you were both supernatural, and both had an affinity for water, but nothing further. It was determined at the time that the only way to know for sure was to wait until you both turned twenty."

"And now? Do you know now?"

He shifts uncomfortably on his seat. His mask is breaking up, but I don't know if he's doing it on purpose to make me think I'm winning somehow. As if this is going to end well for me, whatever he says. "We've had an idea for a long time. The other girl... Liling. She's much bigger and stronger than you. More like a dragon in size."

I blink, trying to take in what he's saying.

He thinks the other girl is a dragon. I let out a breath, so small it's almost a sigh.

I'm not a dragon. *I'm not his daughter.*

"Where is she? Was she raised like me?"

He nods. "She had protectors and SIG agents like you. But her cover was never broken like yours and she had a much more sheltered upbringing."

I hesitate. "Does that mean... You're not my father?"

He shakes his head, looking sad for the first time. "I'm sorry. I don't know who your father is. All I know is that your mother died alongside Xinglong."

I nod and bow my head. I've never had a mother, but I always thought I had a father, no matter how reluctant he might have been. Now I've lost even that much.

I clench my hands in my lap. It doesn't matter anyway. This man never acted like a real father. It was Jeff and Si who raised me, who taught me what I needed to know to survive. I shouldn't be sad to find out that SIG Agent Damien Walker isn't my father. He never really was.

I straighten my shoulders and look back up at him. Waiting.

He takes a breath and glances at the camera above our heads. It's a tiny glance, but I catch it.

I'm not sure, but I think he's trying to tell me something. It's just a pity that I don't know what the hell it is. "What are you going to do with me, now you have me here?"

"Once we've confirmed that Liling is the dragon, we need to determine what kind of supernatural you are, and the level of threat you pose to the security and safety of the world. If you're not high risk, you'll be recruited to the SIG."

"And if I'm dangerous? Or I don't want to work for the SIG?"

"Then you will be... disposed of." He says the words like he's talking about putting the rubbish out at the curb. I guess that *is* what he's talking about.

Again, I try to find some emotion on his face but the mask is firmly back in place. "So if I don't agree to be recruited, you're going to kill me?" I can't believe what I'm hearing. What happened to liberty and democracy for all?

"Jeff never told me you were such a drama queen," he says softly, his hard eyes boring into mine.

I open and close my mouth like a fish. It's the first time he's admitted to any knowledge of my life with Jeff and Si. For a second, all I can see is their familiar faces.

"Don't you dare talk to me about Jeff," I say, practically snarling the words.

He shrugs. "Jeff kept me informed. I can see now that he was glossing over a few personality issues."

For a second, I don't know how to deal with it. But then I hear Jeff's voice in my head. *He's just trying to mess with you. Don't let him get into your head. You're stronger than that.*

And then I'm fine. I let out my breath slowly and look up into Damien Walker's eyes. Holding my hands loosely together in front of me on the table, I smile and say "Thank you for your interest, but I won't be joining the SIG."

He leans back in his chair and smiles back at me. This time with genuine amusement. "Didn't we just establish that you have no choice?"

"I was just letting you know my stance, so you know what to do with me later on. In fact, perhaps you should just get it over with right now?" I glance meaningfully at the gun in the holster under his jacket.

"Don't be too hasty. We have time to discuss a few things. Like who you are, for example."

"And who am I?" I lean back, trying to act casual. My heart is beating a mile a minute. If I'm not a dragon, then I'm not sure it matters.

He leans toward me, his hands clasped together on the table—a mirror of my previous posture. "You are anything you want to be," he says softly, his eyes intent on my face. For the first time, I feel like I'm seeing the real him.

"What if I want to be a hula dancer in the circus?" I say defiantly back. I can feel tears welling in my eyes, and I blink them back.

"It would be a great waste, given your unique talents."

I let out a frustrated breath. "And just what unique talents are those?"

He doesn't even blink at my outburst, just looks at me. There is a long silence. I cross my arms, but don't say anything. I suffer through his uncomfortable silence.

"Jeff taught you well. As did Si. You would be a huge asset to the SIG."

"I don't want to be an asset to the organization that got them both killed."

"That's not quite true."

"What do you mean? Seth had a tracking spell inserted inside him. It could only have come from someone inside the SIG. I *know* it's true, I saw it."

"There's someone I want you to see." He nods to the camera, and the locked door opens again. A man literally falls through the doorway, as if someone has just pushed him.

He's tall, with straight dark hair, warm skin, and almond-shaped eyes. He picks himself up off the floor. He glares behind him at whoever pushed him through the door, but when he turns to face the room and sees me, he freezes.

The blood drains from my body.

Si.

36

I stand up slowly. "I saw them shoot you," I whisper, my voice breaking. "I thought you were dead."

He nods, his eyes filling with tears. "Yes. But I don't have lizard scales for nothing, Mei. You know that."

I run over to him, throwing my arms around his shoulders. Sobbing all over his shirt, I can't control my reaction. He's back from the dead. Si puts his arms up and holds me close, giving me the comfort I need.

I pull back for a moment. A small tendril of hope crawls out of my stomach. "Jeff?" I ask.

He shakes his head sadly. "I'm sorry, little one. I couldn't save him."

I crush my face against his shoulder again and squeeze my eyes shut.

"I hate to interrupt this touching scene, but you're here for a reason, Protector." My father's voice is hard.

Si pulls back a little and holds onto my arms. He looks down into my eyes. "If I'm here, it's because you're not cooperating," he says quietly.

Shaking my head, I try to lean back against him. He resists, holding me at a distance.

"You must do what they say, Mei. It's a matter of life and death. There are nasty people out there in the world, and you can't afford to be without allies. The SIG are powerful allies."

"So I should join the morons who gave away our position to the Earthbound? Who got Jeff killed?"

"It's not possible to be perfect in this life, Mei."

"I don't want to work for them," I whisper. I don't think I have what it takes to be part of an organization like the SIG. They'd want me to follow too many rules, be a certain kind of person. "I'm not a dragon. They don't need me."

"So I hear." He glances at Agent Walker. "However, you will be safer if you are part of the beast, than if you are outside of it."

"Do you really think it's the right thing to do?" I ask. Perhaps I shouldn't be so stubborn. I wipe the tears from my face with one hand and try to think clearly.

"Yes. Absolutely," Si confirms. "It's what Jeff would have told you to do."

Frowning, I peer up at Si. Jeff always said he wished he'd never joined the SIG. It was the last thing he'd want me to do. Si grasps my hands and covertly pushes a folded-up piece of paper into my palm. I try to act casual and pretend nothing is happening.

"You have to take this opportunity with both hands, Mei. It will keep you safe but also give you the skills you need to survive. Just promise me you'll think about it, at least?"

I nod jerkily. Stepping away from Si, I put my hand in the pocket of my shorts. He turns and heads back to the door. It opens and he walks through without a backward glance.

The door slams and the sound echoes around the interview room.

I turn back to Agent Walker. "So what now?" I ask, fingering the paper in my pocket.

"Have you changed your mind about working with the SIG?"

"I need time to think about it," I say, glancing up at the camera.

"Then you can go back to your sleeping quarters. We can do nothing official until you both turn twenty."

"It's not for another few weeks," I say. "You can't keep me waiting around here for that long."

"You turn twenty in exactly one week. We altered the date, so we would be the only ones who knew precisely."

"You changed my birth date?" A lifetime of birthday candles and presents becomes a lie with one casual statement. This day just keeps getting worse.

"Yes." He snaps his fingers at the camera, and seconds later, a new guard comes into the room.

"I had the last man reassigned," says Agent Walker. "I didn't like his attitude."

I'm grateful, but I'm not going to show it. Not now I know whose side he's working on.

"Goodbye, Mei. We'll talk again soon," he says as I'm led out the door by my new guard.

As I head back to my room, I become determined about one thing.

I'm not going to see him again if I can help it.

37

I go straight to the bed and lie down, facing away from the camera. I stay there, curled up and unmoving for at least ten minutes. Long enough for whoever is watching me to get bored and look away.

Putting my hand in my pocket again, I pull out the note, keeping it hidden in my hand. I pass it down to the hand that's lying against the bed, and hold it there against my chest for another five minutes. Luckily, Si taught me the value of patience, because all I want to do is leap up and tear open the piece of paper and figure out what it says.

Eventually, I allow myself to open the folds, until there it is. A note from Si.

Don't worry. Your father is working on getting us out. Just stay where you are. We have a plan.

I re-read it, my hands shaking. He's working with my father? The one who ratted us out to begin with? I crush the note into my palm. My father is working an angle on Si. He's tricked him into thinking he's on our side.

What Si doesn't know is that my father values the SIG

more than he values his own daughter. Except I'm not even his daughter anymore.

I'm just the other baby.

I clench my hand into a fist and roll onto my back, staring up at the metallic ceiling. If I'm going to get out of here, I'm going to have to do it myself. And I need to figure out how to get Si, and maybe Seth, out at the same time. It seems an almost impossible task, and I want to cry with frustration.

I didn't ask for any of this. I don't want to work for the SIG, and I don't want to have unnamed special powers that everyone is trying to use for their own benefit. Everyone except me. Putting my hands on my stomach, I close my eyes, trying to lose myself in an internal world.

Unthinkingly, I reach out for the spell web. Usually that's enough to comfort me, but the absence of the grid in this building is just another jarring reminder that these people are more powerful than I'd ever realized. It makes me feel off balance, and out of step. It also makes me understand how much I rely on the spell web in my everyday life.

The lack of the spell web at the headquarters is another puzzle I want to solve before I leave this place. If it can be taken down or removed in one particular area, then surely the same thing can be done in other places. How come no one has ever heard of it? Do the Earthbound know?

I must be able to access the spell web, even just a little bit? It can't be completely gone. I concentrate hard, locking down all my outside senses and creating a laser-sharp focus inside my head. There's nothing there. The spell web is well and truly hidden.

But as I'm about to retreat, I sense something new. It's a small hot kernel of energy in the depths of my consciousness. I poke at it. Is it something they put inside me when they captured me? Some kind of tracking spell like Seth had?

But when? I haven't been unconscious at any time since they captured us. It feels like forever, but it's really only been hours.

I poke at it a second time, and the ball of energy flares to life. Warmth spreads over my whole body and I can't remember when I've ever felt this good before. Maybe I haven't.

I stretch out on the bed, holding my hands high over my head, and pointing my toes like a dancer. I open my eyes slowly, trying to hold onto the feeling of contentment.

The view before me has changed. Instead of the metallic grey of the walls and ceiling, and the white of the sheets on the bed, all I see is shades of red, orange, and yellow. I blink. The area around the camera in the corner is red, as is the lock on the door. I look down at myself and I'm a vibrant red that almost hurts my eyes. The metal on the roof is a pale, dull yellow.

It takes a few moments for my brain to tick over but then it hits me, I know what's happening. I'm seeing heat signatures. My eyes are translating heat, rather than visual signals for my brain. What does it mean? If I'm not a dragon, what the hell am I? For the first time, I start to wonder if I might not be better off as a dragon. At least I'd know where I stand.

I look around the room, testing out my new ability. Standing up, I attempt to walk around without banging into the walls or the bed. It takes some practice, but eventually I get used to it. A large patch of heat in one corner of the room attracts my attention. Wandering over, I assess what I can see. It's a motor of some kind, maybe the ventilation system. There's a faint whirring noise coming through the metal walls. I put my hand against the metal, testing what my senses are telling me. If I've got new vision, perhaps I have other helpful new skills.

But I can't feel anything more than the vibration.

Huffing out a disgruntled breath, I let my vision switch back to normal, and go back to my bed and sit down. My best hope for getting out of here will be when they take me down the hallway into the interrogation room again.

There must be some way I can overpower the guard, run for my life, and escape. Hopefully grabbing Si and Seth along the way. The very idea is a little overwhelming, but I'm determined to at least try.

In the meantime, there's nothing for me to do, but wait.

Except I've never been much good at waiting.

First I lie facedown on the floor and do one hundred pushups. Then I switch to my back and do sit-ups. It occurs to me that I should be saving my energy, but I'm too restless to sit still. And my body hasn't had a proper workout in days.

I'm just deciding whether to do more pushups or switch to another exercise when the door opens sharply, and a tall, broad man walks in. I sit up, holding my arms around my knees, watching as he stops two yards away from me. He's got a greying goatee and sharp blue eyes that seem to take in and assess everything around him, including me.

"I'm Director Holden of the SIG." He pauses to see my reaction. "I have decided to introduce you to the other woman. The real dragon."

I manage to keep my face blank. "Why?"

He clears his throat. "To compare you side by side. To run some tests."

I tip my head to one side. "I thought you knew she was the one?"

"Just stand and come with me. No more questions."

38

I follow Director Holden down the hallway, past room seven. My guard is holding my arm so tightly, it's as if he knows I'm thinking of escape.

We turn down different corridors a couple times and then arrive at a door already being guarded by a large man in the red and blue SIG guard uniform.

The guard salutes and then opens the door for us.

It's a large gym, with a basketball court taking up the middle of the floor, but with other equipment around the room. Another woman is already there. She's doing a flip over a vault that has been set up with a trampoline at the beginning and a padded mat after it.

"Gym class?" I ask. Not that I've ever been to a gym class, I was never allowed to go to school, or any other organized activities.

"Liling has shown a high level of proficiency in gym activities. She has been training as a gymnast since she was a child." He watches Liling closely, his eyes narrowed.

"Is that a common dragon shifter trait?"

He nods. "Yes. She exhibits many of the dragon characteristics we would expect."

"And I don't?"

He shakes his head. "We have been unable to categorize you. That is why our researchers have requested this series of tests."

"What if I refuse?" I won't be paraded around like a lab rat.

"You have no choice but to do these tests. Your life is at stake."

I shake my head. "I won't do it."

"If you won't do it for your own sake, then think of your friend Si," he says in a silky voice.

He doesn't say the actual words, but the threat hangs heavy in the air between us.

My eyes feel like they're as big and round as saucers. "You can't do this. I have rights! I'm a citizen of this country."

"Actually, you're not. You were smuggled into the US as a baby and never received citizenship of any kind. Added to this, you have been determined to be a threat to national security. You have no rights."

It hits me like a punch in the stomach. To this man, I'm no one. His lack of concern is evident in the way he's speaking to me, and in the bland expression on his face.

"Where's Agent Walker? I need to speak to him," I say desperately.

"Agent Walker cannot make an impartial decision in this matter. He has been reassigned to another case. He left an hour ago."

"What about Seth? What have you done with him?" There must be someone around who's on my side.

"Agent Barnes is going through a debriefing process. He will be reassigned."

It gives me hope that Seth is okay at least. "Can I see him?"

"No, you may not."

The director motions behind him, and two large guards stride into the room. They each grab one of my arms and drag me toward the vault. I wonder what they intend to do? Force me to do flips?

I give a single hysterical laugh before shaking myself out of it.

The director has followed behind me and stands to one side as we wait for Liling to join us. She's taller than I am, with strong shoulders and a serious expression. She has long dark hair like mine, the same almond-shaped eyes and brown irises. We're clearly both of half-Chinese heritage. I try to spot any of Agent Walker's characteristics in her face, but can see nothing that hints of him.

"So you are the other one?" she says. Her voice is musical, soft. She glances at the guards with a frown, but says nothing.

I nod, with a half-smile. It's not her fault that I'm being held by my two guards.

"We are to do some tests?" she asks the director.

"Yes. We wish to see how you both perform next to each other." The director almost sounds differential to her.

I already see why they're sure she's the dragon. She has a commanding presence. She's much bigger than me, taller, more poised. She holds herself like a ballet dancer, despite her size. I wish I could be half as graceful. I tug at the sleeve of my shirt. It makes me feel like the grubby younger cousin.

"Are you going to cooperate?" the director asks.

I nod. I'm fascinated by Liling now. I want a chance to talk to her.

The guards let go of my arms, and I shake them out. Liling nods to me and then leads the way to the vault.

"Have you ever done this before?" she asks gently.

I shake my head. "I can do flips and cartwheels, stuff like that. I use them in fighting."

Her eyes widen at the mention of fighting, but she nods. "I'll show you the move, and how you're supposed to use the vault. Then you can have a try."

"Have you been doing this long?"

"All my life."

I want to keep peppering her with questions, but the director is glaring at us, and Liling seems impatient to get started.

As she's instructing me on the best way to gather momentum, I notice a string of people in white lab coats entering the far end of the gym. They're carrying all sorts of equipment. "I thought he was lying about the researchers," I blurt out.

"Oh no. The director never lies," says Liling.

"How do you know?" I ask with a frown.

"I've lived with him my entire life," she says simply. "I was raised with his family."

My body goes cold. I glance over at the director. What's going on?

Liling doesn't seem to understand the implications of this information, and continues her monologue on how to traverse over the vault in the most graceful manner.

I try to unravel the strands based on this new piece of information and struggle to know where to even begin. Did he lie to Agent Walker about the babies? Did they always know which of us was the dragon?

The thought leaves me breathless. But it feels like there is more going on here than I fully understand. What is the point of having a dragon on a lead? Does he intend to do something with that power?

The director has effectively stolen Agent Walker's daughter out from under the agent's nose, changed her loyalties and her behavior in favor of himself.

I glance at Liling. She's tall, graceful, and strong. Everything I imagine a dragon should be in human form. But she seems strangely docile, accepting of whatever the director throws at us. I have a terrible feeling she will do whatever he tells her to do.

He's got a *dragon* on a leash. Does Agent Walker realize this?

I have a feeling that his reassignment has something to do with the discovery of this fact.

39

My first go at vaulting is an utter disaster.

I run up, jump on the small angled trampoline, as Liling has instructed, and then slam directly into the vault. Hard. The wind is knocked out of my lungs and I dangle there for a moment.

"You didn't angle yourself correctly," says Liling from just behind me. Her voice is like a gentle river flowing over rocks.

It makes me want to punch her. Just a little bit.

Instead, I try again, and again, and again.

"Can we try something else?" I eventually ask in desperation.

"You mentioned being able to do flips?" Liling asks. "Perhaps we can move onto that."

The guards help us haul a few mats together in a long row, and Liling stands at the beginning. She holds her hands high and then pulls them down in some kind of gymnastics move. Then she's off. Every eye in the room is spellbound by her display of coordination and grace.

When it's my turn, I decide to use my fighting moves instead, knowing I can't do the same kind of moves that she displayed. I bow, facing the long row of mats, and let out a breath. My concentration narrows and I focus on the last kata—a series of moves used in karate—that Si had been teaching me before he... well, before I *thought* he died. I step to one side of the mats; I'm not going to use them for this.

I don't really think of anything as I start my kata. It's a chance for me to forget everything else that has been going on. I can focus on my body and doing the moves to the best of my ability. It involves a couple turning leaps that end in kicks, some complicated punches and blocks, and ends on a series of moves that it took me days of practice to learn. Si says I would be a black belt if I'd ever been formally tested.

I land on the last twisting kick, and *kiai* as loud as I can. I don't notice the silence in the room around me at first, but when I look up, everyone is staring, stunned.

Bowing to an imaginary judge, I return to standing at attention. Then I break out of my karate stance. No one has moved. They're all still looking at me like I'm another species. And I guess I am. Not that any of us know what species that might be.

The director takes a step backward. "That's enough for today. Guards, take Mei back to her room."

The guards grasp my arms, although it's looser this time. They understand I'm not as easy to compel as they thought I was, I guess. Not that I'm going to try anything right now.

They lead me out into the hallway, and I try to understand what just happened. Surely watching me do the kata wasn't that life-changing?

"Wait!" The sound of the director's footsteps follows us up the corridor and the two guards stop.

He stands in front of me and swallows. "That... display... back there makes it obvious to me that you are highly dangerous. It has been decided that you will be remanded into the custody of our partner organization, the Earthbound. They have the appropriate facilities to ensure that you are no longer a threat."

My heart leaps into my throat. Locked rooms, water chambers. "You can't do that!" I pause, thinking quickly. "They won't even want me, now they know I'm not a dragon."

"Vincent assures me he still has use for one such as you. And he has promised they will ensure your continued well-being."

"Vincent is lying!" I strain against the arms holding me. "You know he's lying." Then I think about what he's saying.

He's already talked to Vincent and made a deal with the Earthbound leader. The decision to send me right this minute is the only change in a plan that has already been made. The blood is pounding through my veins as I think about going back there to Vincent. "He's already tried to kill me," I say desperately.

"Enough. This is not a discussion." He glances at the guards. "Take her to the transport."

Then he turns and stalks off in the opposite direction.

I struggle, but the two men are strong, and I can't find the leverage I need to escape their grip. I'm not sure without the help of the spell web, but they have to be supernaturals of some sort. They're too strong to be humans.

As I move, something bumps against my chest. The small blue bottle, tied around my neck by a piece of string. For some reason, no one here has guessed just how dangerous it is. The demon inside could beat these two men into the ground without a second thought. The only problem is that he's more likely to come after me first. Just like he did to the pawnshop owner. I'd get the guards dead, but I'd be dead too.

Although... presumably they have ways of dealing with things like demons around here. They wouldn't be a very effective supernatural policing organization if they didn't.

The only problem is how to get the guards to let go of my arm.

I clear my throat. "You're hurting my arms," I say.

They ignore me, continuing to drag me down the hall.

"I can walk on my own, you know. If you'd just slow up and let me gather my feet under me."

Their speed starts to seem suspicious. "Are you trying to get me out of here in a hurry? To avoid someone? Maybe Agent Walker?"

An idea forms in my head. Is this sanctioned? Or is the director acting on his own? I'm suddenly sure that, for whatever reason, the director is working at cross purposes to Agent Walker. There's a power play in action, and I'm stuck in the middle of it.

"Are you allowed to do this?" I say carefully. "I mean, the director told you to do it, so you have to. But is he acting within his powers?"

The guards don't even acknowledge that I've spoken. I sigh. Jeff would have been out of here, with some kind of monetary compensation and a limo to the airport by now.

The thought of Jeff makes me pause, a lump settling in my throat. I swallow back a self-pitying sob. I've been leaping from one crisis to the next since we were attacked, and I can't get a moment to think.

Then I remember Si isn't dead after all. He's here somewhere, working on a plan to get me out.

Perhaps that's the rush. The director wants to get onside with the Earthbound, send them a toy to play with instead of the real dragon, so they'll help with whatever scam he's running.

Although, he *is* the director of the SIG. He can probably just do stuff like this.

We round another corner, and suddenly the corridor is filled with a green gas. I cough and accidentally inhale a small amount of it. It stings all the way down my throat, and I gag instinctually. The hands that were holding me so tightly fall away, and I hear a thump on the ground. I hold my breath, but I've inhaled enough of the green gas to be as susceptible as the guards. Through the billowing green cloud, two men stride toward me, gas masks in place. One of them hands me a mask and I pull it on, taking a relieved gasp of air.

"Come on. We don't have much time," says a voice through the headset in the gas mask. I turn with a relieved smile to Seth. He's grasped my hand in one of his, and he's pulling me along the corridor. Ahead of us, Si is marking point.

"How did you know?" I ask, trying to see through the cloud of gas in the corridor.

"We didn't. At least not until ten minutes ago. The director sped up the timeframes. You weren't supposed to be moved anywhere until tomorrow."

I blink and my heat vision turns on. All I can see are the heat signatures of myself, Seth, and Si, and the small Demon bottle around my neck, which is like the sun compared to everything else.

We sprint around a corner and there's a large red lump in front of us. I blink and my normal vision returns. It's a group of seven agents with gas masks in place and guns aimed directly at us. The director stands in the middle of the agents, his face red and a sheen of sweat on his forehead. He pulls off his gas mask, his face smug. "Did you think we'd be unprepared for your little escape plan?" he says with a sneer. "A junior agent and a lizard? You don't have what it takes to beat me."

I glance at Si. He usually gets riled up over lizard comments. He's a chameleon; there's a difference. But his expression is calm, almost amused under the face plate.

Seconds later, it becomes obvious why. One of the agents behind the director lifts the butt of his gun and slams it into the back of the director's head, knocking him out. He slumps to the floor. I hesitate, glancing between Seth and the other agents across from us who still have their weapons trained in our direction.

As one, they lower their guns, standing down.

One of the men takes off his mask. "Get out of here, Seth. You don't have much time." It's Agent Harkness, the metal worker I saw when I first arrived.

Seth nods. "You won't regret this."

Harkness shakes his head. "I owe Agent Walker. There was never any choice. Now get outta here." He pushes Seth toward the end of the corridor.

And then we're off again, running for all we're worth.

We skid to a halt outside a bank of elevators, and Seth presses the button to take us to the ground.

"Where are we going? How'd you even plan this?" I ask, as we get into the first elevator that arrives, my heart pounding like it's trying to escape my chest.

"We're meeting Walker in the garage and we're getting you out of here," Si tells me. His voice is muffled through the gas mask, and I frown. I put my hand up to pull it off, but Seth stills my movement.

"We need to leave them on until we're out of the building. Just in case," Seth says.

I nod and put my hand back down. We're not out of the woods yet.

40

The elevator doors open to the garage and green gas fills the air.

There's no visibility at all, and we have to make our way through it to whatever vehicle they've found for us. Gun shots ring out all around us. There's a blind shoot-out going on—no one can see what they're firing at, but they're shooting all the same.

Si gestures for us to fall into line behind him. His skin has already changed into the hard scales that protect him in moments like this. We can't see more than a step in front of us, and my pulse is hammering so hard I'm sure they're going to find us just because of the noise.

I blink, and my heat vision is back. I can't see the gas, but I can see the shapes of about five men in front of us. One of them is Agent Walker, and the other four must be SIG agents who were smart enough to put gas masks on before coming to investigate.

"I can see five figures," I whisper into the mask, hoping my voice doesn't carry over the sound of gun shots.

"Where?" Si whispers. I notice he doesn't question how I can see them.

"I think it's probably Agent Walker at about our eleven o'clock. The other shooters are gathered together at about three o'clock." I scan the room. "Wait. There's another man moving slowly around the back."

"That could be Agent Walker as well," Seth says.

I nod in acknowledgement. I don't know who the heat signatures represent.

A gun fires, and I'm staring at it when it goes off. The light blinds me, and for a moment, I can't see anything. I hear the bullet hit flesh close to us, and Si grunts.

"Are you hit? Did it get you?" I whisper frantically at Si, grabbing his arm.

Seth pulls us behind a car and Si follows more slowly.

"It hit my scales. I'm just winded. I'll be fine."

I throw my arms around his neck in a tight hug. "I can't lose you again," I whisper.

He puts one hand on my back. "It's okay. I'm fine, little one."

"We need to hurry," Seth says. "There's not much time."

Si nods. "You two stay here. I'm going after those agents." Si moves off before I can tell him to stop.

Seth has a similar frustration in his eyes.

"Maybe we should help?" I ask. I blink and my normal visions returns.

"How?"

"A distraction?"

Seth frowns. "What do you have in mind?"

I finger the small blue bottle around my neck, but it doesn't seem like a good idea. There's still no guarantee it won't come after me first. "Maybe we could start up a few of these cars? Or..." I glance around me, trying to find something that might work. There's a fire extinguisher behind glass on the walls. "What about using that?" I ask, pointing.

"Can't we just shoot at them? You can see them, can't you?"

I shake my head. "I don't know who is who. There's a chance we'd accidentally shoot Agent Walker or Si." I blink again, and nothing happens. I don't know how to get the heat signature vision back, so I actually have no idea where they are at this moment in time anyway. "We should take them out one by one, like Si."

"It's harder one on one. These guys are professional agents."

I shake my head and lean toward him. "It won't be one on one. It will be two on one. Plus fire extinguisher foam."

He hesitates for a moment, then nods. "Let's do it."

I grin, and he gives a half-smile back.

I blink, and suddenly I'm seeing everything in reds, oranges, and yellows again. It's very disconcerting. "There's someone over there, on the other side of that car," I whisper.

"Let's get the fire extinguisher and find our first victim," Seth says, appearing as a red-orange blob in front of me. He crouch-runs over to the glass box set into the wall and smashes his elbow against the glass. It shatters loudly, in what turned out to be a moment of silence. There's silence for a second, and then bullets start firing in Seth's direction.

But he's already removed the fire extinguisher and is running in a low crouch back to me.

"What now?" I whisper.

"The man behind the car?" he asks quietly, handing me the fire extinguisher.

I nod and follow behind him. We venture out from the protection of the rows of cars, into the space between, and I have to force myself to keep going, despite knowing we're protected by the green gas that's still floating in the air.

I settle with relief back into place beside Seth when we reach the car. It's a Ford station wagon. I can't imagine what the SIG might use it for. Seth points to the back of the car, and I nod. The heat signature is still tucked in behind the back of the station wagon. Seth dodges back around the other side, and I creep forward on this side.

I blink back to normal vision as I count to three and then leap out from the car, spraying the agent in the face. From the other side, Seth knocks his gun out of his hands with a well-aimed kick. I grab for the gun, while Seth punches the guy in the face. The agent screams from the impact, and blood squirts through the foam, turning it a pinkish red.

He curls over and clutches at his face.

"Do we knock him out?" I ask.

Seth pulls some plastic zip ties out of his jacket pocket and wraps them around the agent's legs and hands. The agent resists, but Seth whispers something in his ear, and he stills.

I blink and nothing happens.

"Where now?" whispers Seth.

I close my eyes deliberately and open them again. Nothing.

I blink again, and the heat-vision returns. I let out a breath and look around, trying to find the next agent.

The heat signatures are clustered around one small area now, and I point Seth in the right direction, taking the lead this time. We crawl at the back of the cars, along the concrete wall at one side of the garage area. I blink and my normal vision comes back. I sigh with relief—it's hard to maneuver when you can only see heat.

When we're close to the spot I saw them clustered, Seth and I check under a big black SUV. I encounter the wide eyes of an agent I don't recognize staring back out at me. My heart skips up into my throat, until I notice the duct tape across his mouth, and the rope holding his hands in place.

He's already been subdued.

We crawl to the edge of the car, and I poke my head around the corner. Si is crouching over a second agent, this one unconscious, who now has rope tying his hands and legs to the other agent.

"We got another one back there," I whisper to Si, who nods.

"Walker has taken out one of the others. There are still two out there."

I blink my eyes into heat-vision, getting more confident with it every time. I can see the three other heat signatures. Two of them are close together and writhing about like they're fighting, and a third is closing in on the other two. "Quick, just over there. I think Agent Walker is fighting one of them."

We run toward the back of the garage. The gas has almost completely dissipated, and I can see two men struggling between two SUVs just ahead of us.

Another agent is creeping along one side of a smaller black Audi, and I immediately raise my gun. I hesitate, but when I see him aiming his gun at Agent Walker I pull the trigger.

The agent collapses to the ground, and a spreading stain emerges on his shirt. I'm frozen in one spot, mesmerized by the pool of red around the man lying on the concrete in front of us.

41

"Come on, Mei. We have to go." Seth grabs at my arm, and I jerk back into awareness. Agent Walker is walking toward us, smoothing down his rumpled suit.

"We need a car. Something bulletproof," he says. He heads to a black SUV and opens the door, grinning back at the others. "No need to lock the cars when they're in the SIG building, right?"

He leans down and starts the car using a couple of wires. Without a word, we all climb into the vehicle behind him, Si in the front, Seth and me in the back. I lean wearily on Seth's shoulder, glad to know he's okay and to have him around again.

"Everyone put your seatbelts on, this is going to be a bumpy ride." Agent Walker sounds excited rather than anxious, but I sit up and buckle my belt just in case. I have a strong feeling he's an adrenaline junkie.

The car screeches backward and out of the parking space toward the exit. We're almost there when the door to the stairwell bursts open and SIG agents stream out, shooting at the front of the car as they run toward us. I'm not sure we'll be able to make it out of here with that many agents flowing out the door.

I jerk down below the window, and touch the blue bottle at my neck. Should I let him out? They'll be able to subdue the demon—that's what SIG agents are best at—but it will take them time. Meanwhile, we'll be going fast enough to hopefully get us the hell out of Dodge.

I press the button to lower the window.

"What are you doing?" Agent Walker yells as he squeals the car around a corner. "Trying to get us shot?"

Ignoring him, I open the window enough to throw the small vial outside. As the window goes back up, I see the bottle crash into a thousand pieces on the ground behind us.

The same smoky gas as last time emerges from the broken bottle. We're heading out the exit by the time the demon has fully formed, a couple hundred yards behind us. It turns immediately toward our SUV, its gaze like two molten disks of lava shining out of its head. I can almost smell its desire for revenge, and I can't stop shivering.

But most of the SIG agents are shooting at the demon. They're not stupid; they recognize the greater threat. The demon has to turn back to deal with the agents behind it, or it won't be around to get revenge on me.

My hands are shaking, and I hold tight to the side door as I watch what's happening behind us. I'm sure they'll all be fine. SIG agents are tough. And they deal with demons all the time.

I keep repeating it to myself, even as we speed away down the streets of New York. I don't know how, but Agent Walker seems able to avoid the worst of the congestion, and soon we're just another car in the middle of the city.

"Where the hell did you find a demon?" he asks.

I shrug. "Around." I don't feel like talking to him just yet.

He glances at Si, who shrugs. "I'm not complaining. I just can't believe you had it around your damn neck on a string the whole time."

I lift my hand to my now empty neck. "What else was I going to do with it?" I ask neutrally. "I couldn't leave it for someone else to find."

Agent Walker clearly has nothing to say to this, and concentrates on driving. I sit next to Seth and lean my head on his shoulder again.

I shouldn't be able to, but I slide into sleep.

42

There's a thick liquid all around me, and I'm being pulled down into the darkness. I swim frantically, pushing with everything I have, but something is dragging me backward. The water feels tight and sticky. It's more like slime than water, and I know if I open my mouth and try to breathe, I'm going to die.

So I hold my breath, despite the burning in my chest, and keep trying to swim. Just when I know I'm going to die, I open my eyes and gasp in the sweet fresh air.

A scream dies on my lips, and a door opens on the other side of the room. Seth comes in, his eyes wide with concern.

"Are you okay?" he asks.

"Where are we?" I ask huskily, still half dazed from the dream.

"A motel just outside of Philadelphia."

It's one of the flashier motels I've ever stayed in. The room has two beds, and through another door I can see an en suite. I'm assuming Seth came from the main room.

"How long have I been asleep?"

"A couple of hours. You didn't even wake when I carried you in here."

I nod. "Have Si and Agent Walker talked about what we do now?"

"They're waiting for you. They've been particularly tight-lipped." Seth glowers, and I manage a half-smile. At least they're being consistent.

I sigh and move to dangle my legs over the edge of the bed. I push myself to standing and almost topple over. Seth rushes forward and catches me just in time.

"What's happening?" I ask, panic overriding everything else. Seth helps me to sit back down on the bed.

"I don't know." He turns to the door, and yells, "Agent Walker. Si."

"What are you doing?" I say. He doesn't need to call the others, especially not until I'm able to stand again.

Agent Walker comes through the door first, with Si a close second. They look at me, and then at Seth.

"She can't walk," Seth informs them.

"My legs are just a little weak," I say grumpily. "I'm sure I'll be fine."

Agent Walker crouches down in front of me so we're eye to eye. "I think you're close to changing." He's deadly serious.

"Changing?" I frown. "Into what?"

"Mei, all these years... We were wrong," Agent Walker says. "You're the dragon, not Liling. I realized it when you were in the interview room with me."

If I'd been standing, I would have toppled over again.

I blink a few times, trying to process what he's saying, and miss his next words. "Pardon?" I say, his face blurring in front of me for a second.

"She might be stronger, but you're more wily. Smarter.

You have the intelligence that marks a dragon. And you look like your mother, you have some of her mannerisms. I should have seen it earlier." He reaches up, as if he's going to touch my face, but stops. "I'm so sorry."

A thought occurs to me. "So you're my father again?" I don't know what I want him to say.

He hesitates. "Yes. I'm your biological father. And your mother was a beautiful Chinese dragon named Xinglong." His voice is wistful.

I nod. He's already told me as much. "Am I half-dragon? Because you're my father?" I literally know nothing about dragons except what Vincent told me, and I don't even know if that was true.

He shakes his head. "Dragons and supernaturals are intertwined. Dragons don't mate with other dragons. You're a full dragon. Possibly the last in the entire world."

I let out a breath of air.

I blink, and the room around me turns into reds and oranges and yellows.

I'm a dragon.

43

"From what I've read, dragons spend the last few days before their twentieth birthday changing into a dragon," my father says. It's surprisingly easy to start thinking of him like that again. "It's an extremely vulnerable period. We were expecting Liling to start the process any day." He's pacing in front of the bed where I'm still sitting, swaying slightly.

Goose bumps appear all over my body, and I rub my hands up and down my arms. "It takes days?"

My eyes blur, and I wish Jeff had let me in on his suspicions a few years earlier. I mean, I assume he figured it out long before the others, based on his little box of treasures. Perhaps if he'd shown me his wooden box a couple of years ago, I would have been able to read through it and get used to the idea.

What the hell was he thinking?

I could have been more prepared. I could have been better able to deal with the idea that my body shape is going to change from a smaller-than-average supernatural woman to a sodding enormous dragon in the next few days. My brain can't even comprehend how that is going to work.

I think it's going to involve a lot of pain. My hands clench on the bedspread.

"It's the final part of becoming a dragon. After you go through the change, you'll be a full dragon, with your full powers."

"Will I be in dragon...shape...from then on?"

Shaking his head, my father crouches down in front of me. "You'll be able to switch from your human form to your dragon form at will. Don't worry, it doesn't have to change your life. Not completely." He reaches out and takes my hands. I'm feeling too surprised to do anything other than let him. The blank face he presented at SIG headquarters is gone, and in its place is a painfully raw emotion that wavers between fear and hope. A moment passes and I try to move my hands away, but can't. The immobility of my legs is moving out into other areas of my body.

"I've been waiting for this day for a long time," he says softly.

"I haven't, because no one fucking told me," I grind out. My mouth feels like it's full of cotton.

He tightens his grip on my hands. "That was a mistake. I see that now. But I honestly didn't know which of you was my daughter in the early days. And then later, we thought Liling was the dragon, so all I would have told you was that you weren't a dragon."

I'm somewhat mollified by that admission. "Jeff knew. Or at least guessed. He left me a box of information on dragons in Quincy."

My father's eyes sharpen on my face. "He did? Then he was smarter than I realized." He pauses. "Where's the box now?"

I glance over at Seth. "We mailed it. Before we went to see you."

My father frowns. "You didn't need to do that. I would have kept it safe."

I raise my eyebrows at him. "Really? Cause from where I'm sitting, it looks like you double-crossed us."

"You know... You know it had to be done that way, don't you? I really didn't know which of you was the dragon, despite our assumptions."

"What would have happened to me if I hadn't been the dragon? Or if you hadn't realized in time? Would you have let the director send me to the Earthbound?"

He hesitates. "I would have tried to help you. Where I could."

It's the answer I was expecting. It makes sense that the most important thing to my father is the baby dragon, the daughter he had with my mother. I just didn't expect it to hurt so much. I want him to care about me, whether I'm the dragon or not. I swallow over the sudden lump in my throat and look up at Seth. The expression on his face is enough to let me know that Seth would have helped me, no matter what.

I let out a tired breath. I'm expecting too much of my father, I know that. It's not fair to ask him to care about a child that might not have been his.

But some irrational part of me just can't help it.

I glance down to my legs, and the hands that are now immobile next to them. "Will I be like this until I change?"

My father nods. "I think so. We have to get you to a secure location."

"Where?"

"I found an old dragon nesting ground during my

research. You should be safe there while you succumb to the change."

His mention of the nesting ground reminds me of the cryptic message my father gave Seth at the training school. "Why did you pick Seth? Why did you give him that warning, if you didn't think I was the dragon?"

My father hesitates. "I guess I wasn't as sure as I thought I was," he said, running one hand through his hair. "Jeff was insisting we needed a particular type of replacement for him. The Earthbound were always chasing you, and they seemed so sure. I was hedging my bets, making sure you would be protected, just in case we were wrong." He gives a wry smile. "Turns out it was the right decision."

I can't think of anything to say.

Tires screech outside the motel and we all look up. Seth strides over to the window and twitches the curtains aside. "Five SIG vehicles. They've found our car in the next door motel's parking lot." He glances at my father. "The SUV must have had a tracking system other than the GPS we disabled."

Si swears angrily. "We should have double-checked."

My father stands up, pulling a set of keys out of his pocket, and hands them to Seth. "There's a small van around the back. Painted baby blue. There's money and other supplies in the glove compartment. Take Mei, get her out of here." He pulls another piece of paper out of an inside pocket. "Here are the directions to the nesting ground. Get her there, and she'll be safe. For now at least."

Seth glances at me and hesitates.

"Hurry," my father urges. "I don't have time for you to second-guess me." He pushes Seth in my direction. I glance at Si, but he's nodding in agreement with my father. The pair of them have obviously been talking about this.

Seth's gaze locks with mine, but I can only shrug. I can't help anyone right now. My arms hang limply at my sides, and I feel like I'm about to fall sideways in the bed.

It's terrifying.

"Wha' you goin' to do?" I ask my father, my words slurring.

Seth puts his hands under my arms and knees. He hefts me up into his arms and my head lolls onto his shoulder.

My father practically pushes him out the bedroom door to the back entrance of the motel room. There's another parking lot this way. I can see a baby blue van parked at the far end.

"Si and I will hold them here for as long as we can," my father says. "You need as much of a head start as you can get. You *must* get to the nesting ground. There's too much at stake, too much riding on Mei surviving this, for us to back out now." He rests one hand on my shoulder for a moment before stepping away.

Seth nods once, firmly. "I will, sir."

"Wha' you talkin' about?" I'm confused and frustrated, most especially because Seth is carrying me away from my father, just as he's telling me information I'm certain is important. And where's Si? I've only just gotten my mentor back; I can't leave him again like this. My eyes are almost the only part of my body still working, and I look around frantically. "Si?"

Si moves into my line of sight. He pats my arm and nods. "Just remember what I've taught you, little one."

Tears well in my eyes, and I struggle to understand what's happening. My brain isn't working properly; it feels like everything is in slow motion.

"You must survive, Mei," my father says. "The fate of the world is riding on your shoulders." Then he closes the door, and we're running across the parking lot to the baby blue van.

I scrunch up my face, struggling to remember my father's words.

Why is the fate of the world riding on my survival?

I'm completely unable to move my body now, so Seth buckles me in. I slump to one side, but there's no time to fix my position. He jumps in the driver's seat and the engine starts on the first try, so I know Si's been working on it. We slowly make our way out of the parking area and onto the main road. Behind us I can hear the sound of sirens and a gathering SIG presence at the motel next door.

I don't look back. Truth be told, my head can't actually move in that direction any more.

But I can still look to one side at Seth as he peers over the steering wheel into the dark night ahead of us. Before my eyes loll shut, I'm able to think one last thought.

I'm glad he's here with me.

WHAT'S NEXT?

★★★★★ "I just LOVE this series and can't wait for the next book."

Thank you so much for reading about Mei's adventures.

What will happen next to Mei and Seth? What's going to happen to Mei when she transform into a dragon? And why is it so important to the world that she survives?

Find out in the next book in the series, Searching Dragon. Turn the page to find out more....

Being a dragon is easy... said no one ever.

Especially when your enemies won't cut you any slack.

In fact, it's a complete nightmare.

I've almost killed Si and Seth multiple times. I've almost killed myself a couple times too. Even worse, my enemies have figured out the one way to guarantee that I'll leave the safety of my lair.

They've kidnapped my father.

I mean, don't get me wrong, he's not perfect. But he's the only dad I've got, and I'm determined to get him back.

If only I could figure out how to fly... or even just walk with my new dragon legs.

Searching Dragon Excerpt

The car screams down the road.

Again.

Seth's foot is jammed firmly against the accelerator, but I'm floating away. I feel disconnected from what's happening around me.

All I know is that my nest is close, so close, and I don't know if I'm going to make it.

I can't move my body, although Si is holding me up from the backseat. Before, I could tell he was touching me, but now I can't feel it. My whole body is numb, like it's not connected to me anymore, and my vision is starting to fade.

Everything feels like it's closing down; my body is shutting itself off. We're so close, I can feel it calling to me.

But not close enough.

We screech to a halt on the road about half an hour from the original coordinates.

"Does that look like the mountain in the image she put in our heads?" Seth asks Si.

"Yes. That's it."

"But how do we get there?" asks Seth, his voice slightly panicked.

"We run."

As Seth pulls me out of the SUV, I catch a dim glimpse of a massive glowing area near the coastline. A series of tall rocky hills are coated in the glowing grid of the spell web, pulsing with energy. I don't understand how that can even be possible—I've never seen anything like it before.

Between the road and the glowing hills is rugged, rocky

terrain with a thick forest coating any patches that would otherwise have been easygoing. It's not going to be an easy run, and they'll have to carry me the whole way.

Added to that is the fact that the sun is baking down on us.

But neither of them complain. Seth takes me up in his arms first, and my body flops against his chest, my head bumping in time to his steps. The scent of gunpowder and spice hit my senses, along with sweat and fear. I try to concentrate on where we're going, but my brain is getting foggy. My body feels like jello and I can barely keep my eyes open.

It might already be too late.

When I close my eyes, Seth jerks me awake again. "No sleeping now, Mei. You have to stay awake until we get there."

I blink twice, slowly and carefully. He's right; if I go to sleep now, it's the last of me gone. If I'm not in the nest at that point, I won't make it. I don't know why I'm so sure of this, but I am.

I manage to keep my eyes open and stay focused on the craggy peak ahead of us. When Seth starts running, my vision becomes blurry, the hills turning into green and grey blurs. Maybe Seth can feel the life seeping out of me, just like I can. Or maybe it's just intuition.

Whatever it is, I'm grateful. The edges of my mind are becoming ragged, like something is eating at them. The world is swirling in front of me, my vision almost gone.

I feel every intake as Seth gasps for breath, his chest rising and falling against my body. I taste the salt on my lips from the tears that dried there earlier.

"Here, give me a turn," Si says gruffly from behind us.

Instead of arguing, Seth turns and hands me over. He's exhausted; he would never have stopped if he wasn't.

Si has a stronger grip, and he's a chameleon at the height of his powers. He takes off at a run, using his magic to keep us safe. I hear rather than see his chameleon skin come out over his body, the tiny scales making him stronger.

As Si's magic hums around us, it occurs to me that maybe I could do something with the spell web to help. I try to send my energy along the grid toward Si, like I did back at the beach, but nothing happens. I'm so weak, I can't even use the spell web.

Si jumps from one boulder to the next in a particularly difficult patch of terrain, and my head lolls to one side. I can see down my body, and for the first time I realize that my glowing section of grid has dimmed to almost nonexistent. My head lolls back again. I can't even work up the energy to be worried.

Up ahead, I see the large patch of rocky terrain covered in the spell web.

A painful yearning fills my body, and if I could have gasped at the sheer agony of it, I would have. Now that I'm within range, the nesting ground is somehow calling to me, trying to drag my soul toward it. I have a feeling of being in two places at once, and I start to tremble all over, my body reacting to the pull from the nest.

"I'll take over at the base of the mountain," Seth says.

I don't hear Si's answer; it's lost in the roaring sound that's rushing through my ears.

We're near the base of the ranges where the nest is hidden when my body starts to jerk and my mind is filled with painfully bright flashes of light.

Is this it? Are we too late?

One second, Seth's fierce hazel eyes are gazing down at

me and I'm caught in their depths. Then next second, I don't know where I am. All I can see are fast-moving streaks of light, heat and pain. I can't feel my body, only a burning, blistering heat like the center of a fire.

Is this what it means to be a dragon?

Because so far, it feels like crap.

Then the tingling fear sets in. Have we made it close enough to the nest for me to change? Or will I die, just at the edges?

A gnawing pain fills me, and I don't know if it's my emotions, the fear and the terror so powerful they're climbing up out of my body like a physical thing, or if it's part of the transformation. My breaths are coming in tight, uneven gasps and I feel like I can't get enough air. Do dragons even breathe air?

Why did no one ever tell me what I was? Or prepare me for the nightmare of changing?

It's too much. I can't do it.

And then suddenly, we're there. At the nest. There's a bubbling, boiling, heat-filled connection that I feel immediately. Some tenuous connection back to the real world makes my eyes open. All around me I see flames, an enormous fire burning bright, licking at my body like a lover thought long lost.

One name fights to the top of my consciousness. *Seth.*

I look up and see him as he places me at the center of the flames. His arms are blistering, his face contorted in pain, but he's there with me. Behind him, I see Si pulling him backward out of the fire, Si's chameleon scales covering his whole body.

Then the world becomes nothing more than the flames and the heat. I'm part of the bright, burning fire, my whole being focused down into one speck. Power surrounds me, roaring and raging at my inability to understand what it's saying.

My own magic surges, like a tsunami of power determined to hit the shore, surely enough to take on this raging beast confronting me.

As the two powers strike, there's a terrible explosion, and I'm surrounded by white light and scalding pain. Fire and heat, burning up the air all around.

A tiny part of me wonders how Seth and Si could have survived it.

Another part knows there's no way they could have.

Hi, I'm Trudi Jaye. Now that you've read all the way to the back of the book, I figure you deserve a treat...

How about the story of how Mei's parents first met?

Set twenty-some years ago, this is the story of the first encounter between a hot-shot young SIG agent named Damien Walker and the mysterious woman who knew just how to distract him from his mission.

Don't miss out... There are details in this story that Mei doesn't even know!

Go to my website to get your free short story:

www.trudijayewrites.com

Books by Trudi Jaye

Dragon Rising Series

Hidden Dragon

Searching Dragon

Fighting Dragon

Cursed Dragon

Warrior Dragon (coming soon)

Elemental Witch Series

The Trouble with Magic

The Problem with Witches

The Danger with Demons

Demon Hunter in Hiding Series

Secrets & Demons

Agents & Demons

Magic & Demons

Dragons & Demons

Spells & Demons (coming soon)

Firecaller Series

Fire Mage

Royal Mage (coming soon)

Dark Carnival Series

Ringmaster

The Gift

Tilly's Secret (Free for people who join my mailing list)

High Flyer

Hidden Magic

Shadow Prophecy

Hi! I'm Trudi Jaye. I'm from New Zealand, where I currently live on a beautiful rural property surrounded by horses and cows (not mine!) with my lovely husband and my cheeky eleven-year-old daughter.

I've been writing since I was a kid, and for ten years I worked as a magazine writer and editor, on topics ranging from hardware and electronics to holidays, recipes and university-level research projects.

Now I write novels full time.

I enjoy yoga, although I'm not very bendy, and karate, although I don't like the idea of hitting anyone.

Printed in Great Britain
by Amazon

24690328R00155